I0589858

undeniable

FATE

MIA LONDON

Undeniable Fate
by Mia London

This is a work of fiction. Names, characters, places and incidents either are the product of the author's imagination or are used factitiously, and any resemblance to actual persons, living or dead, business establishments, event or locales is entirely coincidental.

Copyright ©2017 Mia London

All rights reserved. No part of this book may be reproduced or utilized in any form or by any means, electronic or mechanical, including photocopying, recording, or by any information storage and retrieval system, without permission from the publisher.

ISBN - **978-0-9832474-1-8** (ebook)
IBSN - **978-0-9832474-2-5** (pbook)

Publisher: Mia London
PO Box 93852
Southlake, TX 76092

Cover design by Just Write Creations.

Acknowledgements

To Traci and Alla.
I appreciate your boundless talent.

Chapter 1

LILY FIDGETED WITH her tablet cover from her first class seat, chewing the lipstick off her lips. She wasn't afraid of flying, but feared this would be her last trip to Rome. Once the assignment was complete, she'd return to LA and a pink slip, and there wasn't a damn thing she could do about it.

Her company, ALK, had recently been taken over by a larger company—a company known for bringing in their own people and eliminating duplication. Her sadness only grew because she loved her job. Really *loved* her job.

Dammit!

She'd need to remember what her best friend, Courtney, told her. *There are no good ways to be fired, only better ways to accept it. You are smart and good at what you do. Handle it all with grace. You will rock your next job.*

The plane pushed off from the gate, and Lily was secretly thankful that the seat next to her remained vacant.

She ate an egg white omelet and fruit with a cup of black coffee. When the flight attendant offered her a danish, she declined. Carbs were not her friend.

The plane had a scheduled stop in Dallas for those not going through to Rome, so Lily checked her email and waited for passengers to deplane and board.

A tall man dressed in a tailor-made dark suit and blue silk tie boarded. She couldn't determine exactly how tall, but he had a few inches over Kirk, her ex. She crossed her fingers that he'd take the seat next to her. He was likely married, knowing her luck, but he'd be good eye candy for the long flight.

Her stomach tumbled over when he smiled and made his way through first class to her aisle.

"Hi."

"Hi."

He slipped off his suit jacket and hoisted his carry-on suitcase into the overhead compartment. Then, he shoved his leather laptop bag beneath the seat in front of him. His moves were sure and strong, and Lily became captivated watching him.

Although first class gave more space, when Lily inhaled, she was rewarded with a tantalizing musky, masculine scent. Simply divine. If she knew for certain it would go unnoticed, she'd lean in closer.

The man offered polite small talk, and seemed to be in work mode. That's what she called it when her father came home from work, but still had things processing in his brain.

She watched his intense eyes and his sculptured lips when he asked if she had enough leg room. He had a rich, soothing voice she could listen to all day.

Her heart beat faster than normal just being close to him.

When the tall, blonde flight attendant wearing a perfect smile came back to take drink orders, she asked him first. Lily was floored when the man next to her turned and said, "What would you like to drink?"

"Um, a glass of unsweetened tea." The flight attendant blushed at her misstep, but smiled an apology, and then looked at him.

"Ice water with a slice of lime, please."

The attendant returned shortly and set the drinks on the tray tables. The moment he had permission to use his laptop, he opened a rather impressive machine. He focused on his work, typing fast, with an occasional grunt or sigh.

Lily leaned forward to retrieve a book from her bag, and discreetly glanced at his left hand to see he wasn't wearing a ring. Surely someone this handsome and intriguing is married, she thought. Probably engaged.

She sighed and opened her book. After reading for a while, Lily thought about what she needed to accomplish while in Rome, and stewed over her ex. Kirk had wooed her and she'd foolishly fallen for it. She knew his manipulating type, and should have been on guard. She mentally shook her head. *Lessons learned.*

Lily dozed off for about an hour of the twelve-hour flight, and when she awoke the man next to her was sleeping. He'd put his computer away and loosened his tie. She took in his striking features—chiseled jawline, his refined cheekbones, not to mention the tailored cut of his pants.

As if sensing her attention, he opened his eyes and found her looking at him. Her face heated with embarrassment when he grinned at her.

"Good evening," he said, sounding as cultured and polished as he looked.

"Evening. Sorry about that." She turned to face front.

"It's okay. I'm glad I wasn't drooling."

She couldn't hold back her smile.

The flight attendant came to their aisle this time asking them both, "Can I get you anything to eat or drink?"

Lily ordered a glass of white wine, and he asked for a light beer and some nuts. He faced her and introduced himself. "I'm Brandon Morgan."

She shook his hand, noticing how firm yet smooth it felt. "Lily Bennett."

Brandon watched Lily as he gave her his name but it didn't seem to mean anything to her. And for that, he was thankful. Sometimes it was nice to be known as the president and CEO of a Fortune 1000 company, and other times he appreciated the anonymity. Like his two sisters, Brandon had been an Executive Vice President for his father's company, Laurel Medical Incorporated. When his father had a heart attack and triple bypass surgery two years prior, they were forced to take over—earlier then he had expected.

Lily's shoulder-length brunette hair moved slightly when she spoke, and her smile showed in her blue eyes. He instantly appreciated the glimpses of her figure hiding under her suit jacket.

"So, what brings you to Rome, business or pleasure?"

"Business. I'm a project manager for a skincare company based in LA, so this is strictly a business trip," she said without much of a smile.

Didn't she like her job?

"What brings you to Rome?" she parroted.

"Business as well. My company is thinking of buying another company based there."

"Oh wow. So, you're in mergers and acquisitions?"

"Yes, something like that." *And many other things.*

"Exciting. What's the name of the company—"

"This is not the same chardonnay I had earlier." The raised voice from the man in front of them carried throughout the triple-seven's first class.

The flight attendant's eyes widened and she replied in calm tones, though Brandon couldn't make out her words.

"Well, then let me see what else you have," he demanded.

She nodded, giving him a sugary-sweet smile, and flipped her over-dyed hair as she returned to the front of the plane.

Brandon glanced at Lily who had an exaggerated look of surprise on her face.

She giggled softly, and he smiled back.

"Do you go to Rome often?" he asked.

She nodded. "Yes, about twice a year. We grow the ingredients for our skincare a few miles outside of the city."

What is the cost for such a venture? "You can't grow them in the US?"

"The owner has sensitive skin and insisted every product from day one be *uber* organic, you might say. From the seed to the shelf, every process is organic and uncontaminated, and European countries are better equipped to meet our strict requirements."

Interesting. He nodded slowly, recalling she was a product manager, he asked, "And you check up on these farms?"

"Yes, plus I need to oversee the process for a new oil-control face lotion we are about to introduce." She gestured with her hands.

Brandon was drawn to Lily's enthusiasm. That kind of zest and intelligence wasn't often present in employees who'd been doing a job for a long time. "Fascinating."

"It is. It's a great company, and I like my job a lot." He noticed the slight furrow in her brow.

In an obvious subject change, she asked, "Can you talk about your big merger?"

He smiled at the tone in her voice, like she might be privy to a big secret. "Sure. We manufacture medical devices. And this is a friendly buyout. It's a mid-size company that not only gives us instant entry into Europe, but they have a successful product we want to market as well."

The flight attendant returned to take their dinner orders. The frequency of her visits, although he knew it was her protocol, was becoming annoying. He'd much rather talk with Lily than order fish or chicken.

Brandon couldn't have asked for better company. He actually thought he'd use the time to get a chunk of work done.

Lily seemed quiet at times, yet animated and engaging at others. For the remainder of the flight, they talked about their families, Italy, other European countries, latest medical news, nutrition, just about anything and everything. He could laugh because it felt very much like a date.

When they arrived in Italy, he was slightly disappointed to say goodbye to Lily Bennett.

"Nice chatting with you, Brandon." She held out her hand and smiled.

He squeezed her hand and returned the smile. "You too, Lily. Take care of yourself." Then she navigated her rolling suitcase past baggage claim, and he watched her spellbinding curves walk out to a waiting taxi.

Chapter 2

LILY DROPPED HER toiletry bag on the sleek vanity, and glanced at the image in the mirror. Her makeup had faded some, and her brown waves settled too.

Finding a new job equal to what she had at ALK would be hard, she knew. She'd fought to hide her anxiety from the perceptive man beside her. Complaining about getting laid-off was, well, . . . made it somehow real. She didn't want to give up hope that maybe she'd get to keep her job. Despite that, their conversation had been one of the best she'd had with a stranger on her many flights to Rome.

And Brandon was delicious. Oh yes. He stirred something deep inside her, something she hadn't been aware of in quite some time. Even with Kirk. *Especially* with Kirk.

After she showered and smoothed lotion over her skin, she slid on her favorite silky white robe, hoping to relax and clear her jet-lagged, foggy brain. She fluffed the pillows and settled into the hotel's comfy bed. She opened her book, thinking reading would make her drowsy, but her mind continued to stray to Brandon, to his deep voice and intense chocolate eyes. And those perfect lips. The fantasy of those lips on her body brought a flood of heat to her skin and lower parts.

Brandon was as handsome as a European model—smoldering eyes and strong jaw, but it was those lustful thoughts that kept her awake when she needed to rest. She had a facility tour and several meetings the next day, so quality sleep was paramount.

She exhaled, fighting a losing battle. There was only one solution. Release the excess hormones so she could get to sleep, and forget about Brandon.

Lily eased open the dresser drawer, and buried beneath folded clothes, she claimed her vibrator. She laid her white robe on the bed and climbed back in between the sheets. She reminded herself to keep the moaning to a minimal for the walls in the old, fully-renovated hotel seemed rather thin.

She switched off the bedside light and let her hotel room go dark. She started her vibrator on low and let the hum work its magic. Her heartrate increased as she pictured Brandon holding her vibrator for her, doing delectable things to her. In fact, he would be better. He would kiss her and whisper compliments in her ear that Kirk could never seem to appreciate.

Stop! Stop thinking about the asshole.

She brought her mind back to Brandon, and how his mouth and hands would wander her naked body as he easily brought her to climax.

She was close to the edge, when she heard the person next door try and use the key to open the hotel room door. God, it was a little loud, but no worries. Her trusted vibrator never let her down.

Another click. She stopped when it occurred to her that the sound was so loud because it was *her* hotel door opening. *Holy shit!*

She leapt from the bed and whipped her robe around her just as the overhead light went on. She vaguely heard the vibrator roll on the floor but her heart thumped in her chest so hard, she feared she'd go into cardiac arrest.

How loud can I scream?

Brandon yanked his suitcase across the threshold, raised his head, and froze in place.

"Ohmigod. It's you."

"Oh." He scanned the room. "Sorry. Crap." His brow furrowed as he glanced down at his key card. "I'm . . . I think they put me in the wrong room."

Seriously. She gripped the neck of her robe tighter. Her heartrate slowed as her brain processed that someone hadn't just broken in to rape or rob her.

Breathe. "Yes, it would appear so."

His gaze traveled down the length of her.

Shit! Her nipples probably poked against the white satin fabric. He appeared to be having a hard time processing this mix up as much as she because he said nothing. Nothing. He just looked at her.

She wrapped her arms across her chest. "Um, maybe you should go down to the front desk, Brandon, and let them know that you need another room."

"Yes. Definitely." He subtly shook his head. "Yes. I'm sorry about this. I've scared you and interrupted your sleep. I apologize."

"No need. It's not your fault." She took a step closer—to show him to the door or to breathe in his scent, she couldn't be sure.

Brandon stared down at the keycard. "How did this happen?" he asked the universe. He looked up and his lips lifted into a funny grin. "It's weird that I walked into your room. Of all places." He chuckled softly.

She smirked. It was true. Of all the *wrong* rooms to walk into, he'd walked into hers.

His eyes darkened as he scanned her body again. A blush filled her cheeks. She wore nothing beneath that robe. Could he tell she'd been thinking about him?

"Well, it was nice to see you again, Lily."

"You too, Brandon."

He twisted his body and gripped the handle on his carry-on suitcase, but stopped quickly to look her way. "Would you like to have dinner with me tomorrow night? I feel bad about this."

"Um—"

"Please let me make it up to you. You know they have some of the world's best pasta in Rome," he said with a broad smile.

She guffawed because an image of Kirk, eyeing her as she scooped extra parmesan over a plate of spaghetti was the first image that popped in her head. "I'll take you up on dinner, but I'll stick with a salad."

His eyebrows pinched together. "You don't like pasta?"

"I love pasta. My ex said I should stay away from it." The words came out before she could block them. Brandon did not need to hear the sordid details of what her ex thought about her and her eating habits. She bit her lips between her teeth.

He tipped his head. "Okay. Why?"

"Never mind."

"Is it a gluten thing?"

Crap! Her head drooped for a split second. No good way to get out of this. "He said I put on weight too easily."

Brandon's eyes went wide. "He said that to you?" His voice pitched on the last word.

"Yes," she mumbled. *Could this be any more embarrassing?*

She wouldn't consider herself overweight, but definitely curvy. Slightly obsessed, Lily worked out regularly and had strong muscles. Regardless, she couldn't rectify the number she saw every morning on the scale.

"No wonder you dumped the bastard."

Lily let the corner of her lips curve upward. She didn't have the guts to tell Brandon that Kirk had dumped *her*.

His eyes narrowed. "Did he say you were fat?"

Shit! Really? She unknowingly sucked in her stomach. The most handsome man she'd ever met was standing six feet in front of her, wearing his suit with his shirt and tie loosened, and a five o'clock shadow that made her want to run her fingertips along his jawline. She stood naked in just a thin silky robe, and he wanted to have a psychology session?

She couldn't answer so she glanced away. Kirk had said that once, but thankfully never again. He'd made her feel *more* self-conscience of her weight with his pointed stare at almost every meal.

Brandon let go of his luggage and took two steps closer. "From what I saw, your body is pretty amazing. I think your ex needs to have his head examined. That and be exiled to a deserted island with only rice cakes and raw broccoli to eat."

Lily's chuckle turned into a laugh. She actually loved that idea.

He smiled and took another step closer, never breaking eye contact. He stood so close to her now, he could effortlessly reach out and touch her.

She licked her lips, her mouth suddenly dry, and tipped her head up to meet his gaze. His eyes appeared darker than she remembered, like rich espresso.

He offer his hand, palm up, and she hesitated . . . not scared, as much as unsure what he wanted. She released the death-grip on the lapels of her robe and rested her left hand in his. He slowly brought it to his mouth and kissed her knuckles, not once, but twice.

The warmth of his hand and the sensation of his kiss shot low-level electric waves throughout her body. Her lower belly clenched and she nearly moaned.

He stretched his right hand forward, as if he wanted to touch her.

"May I see for myself?" His rich, soothing voice felt like a caress over her.

What! He wanted to see her naked body? The wetness that had threatened to escape at the apex of her thighs with his kiss, no longer held back. Her heart jackhammered in her chest, and she licked her lips.

"I promise not to touch you."

This man she'd only just met, the object of her fantasies, wanted to see her naked. He promised not to touch, and she wanted to say *I don't mind if you do.*

Was she crazy? Had she lost her mind, to even consider his request?

Maybe so, but how often does a man like this even give a girl like me a second look?

Slowly, so slowly, she released her right hand and slid the tips of her fingers down to the sash holding the robe together. Brandon's breath spiked. She watched him as he watched her, his eyes deep pools of chocolate. She untied the sash and let the robe fall apart. Her nipples peaked as she dragged each half of the fabric to the side of her body, fully revealing herself. Her breasts grew heavy.

Brandon inhaled sharply. "Geezus. You're beautiful. Your ex is a fucking idiot."

She averted her eyes. "Please don't say that if you don't mean it."

"Lily." His finger lifted her chin, his thumb brushed her lower lip. "I'm not lying. I mean every word. Your body is perfect."

She shook her head and tugged at her robe with her free hand. "My hips are wide, and my breasts are too big, they're starting to sag."

His eyebrows shot up. "These are the breasts and hips of a woman." He traced a finger over the fabric at her hip, igniting her skin. "A beautiful, curvy woman. Gee-zus."

She bit on her upper lip as he lifted her hand to kiss the back. Then he lowered her hand to her waist and hooked her fingers around the robe's edge, his body heat radiating against her.

"Would you please?"

Holy crap! This may be the most erotic thing she'd ever done. And his obvious desire only fueled her own. Her heavy breasts ached to be caressed.

With his hand over hers, she peeled back the fabric of the robe, slowly revealing her backside. He took several steps to walk behind her, gaining a better view. Her lungs worked for air. She forced her focus to the art on the wall and the brass handles on the dresser.

"Fuck! You have the most amazing heart-shaped ass, Lily."

She blushed for the thousandth time, and peeked over shoulder. "Thank you," she whispered.

His eyes traveled back down the length of her body, before lowering her robe. He glanced in the direction of the bed. His eyes darkened and his face read serious as he looked back at her.

"What is it?" Her head turned and there it was, laying in front of the nightstand—her pink vibrator, the perfect replica of a male penis. She gasped, certain the blood had drained from her face. She tried to pull her robe closed, but he didn't release her left hand.

"Lily, were you using that tonight?" his voice rasped.

She couldn't look at him. *Oh crap.* She was embarrassed, but turned on to immeasurable heights.

"Were you thinking about your ex tonight?"

God, no! She shook her head.

He inched closer toward her, the heat from his body scorching hers. She shivered. "Were you thinking about me tonight while you were using that on yourself?"

Breathe. Speak. "Yes," she managed to squeak out.

"That is the hottest thing I've ever heard." His voice rasped and his breath softly pushed the hair on the top of her head.

15

Really? Wow.

He brought her hand to his lips. She felt a small stutter, almost like he contemplated placing that kiss someplace else. Her eyes fell closed on their own accord. She was really starting to love those lips of his—on her hand, on her *everywhere*. His slow, sensual kisses brought an ache to her sex. She squeezed her legs together.

"Did you get to come, or did I interrupt you?" he asked in a deep silky tone.

"Um, you came in before I could."

He peered at the vibrator again, then looked back at her. "A woman has needs," he cajoled. "Let me help you."

The slightest trickle glided down her inner thigh. Her heart skipped a beat.

"Uh—"

"You can say stop at any time, and I promise I will leave right after. Let me help you come. Let me see you come." His hot breath fell over her hand, and he planted several more slow kisses across her skin.

She wanted to moan. What if she could pull her body flush against his, and feel his strong arms wrap around her? What would it feel like to have those soft lips on hers? To feel his hands explore her?

She swallowed. "Okay," she breathed. She agreed because, God help her, she needed it. The ache at her sex was unbearable. This handsome, sexy man found her attractive and promised to make her feel good. She felt powerless to say no.

He smiled, kissed her hand one last time, and led her to the bed. He switched on the lamp on the bedside table, and for the first time, she could see his erection, straining against his suit pants.

He yanked all the covers back, resting them at the foot of the bed, and he patted the bed for her. She lay down close to the center, and closed her robe.

Silly woman! He's already seen everything.

He switched off the overhead light, shrugged out of his jacket, yanked off his tie, and laid them over the back of the chair. His moves like a confident jaguar, pacing each movement.

"Comfortable?"

"Yes." As much as a woman could be when she was dying for an orgasm so badly if she didn't have one she'd implode.

His dark eyes glowed with a fire from inside. "Great. Just relax. And again, tell me to stop at any time if you're uncomfortable."

"Mmmhmm." There was no way in hell she would stop him. She'd passed her comfort zone the moment his lips touched her hand.

His long fingers grazed her leg and back down again. Then he gently took the edges of the robe resting at her stomach and slowly drew the fabric open, across her breasts, and off to each side of her. A sigh escaped. Her nipples grew taut at the sensation.

"You have gorgeous nipples for those gorgeous breasts," he said as his fingertips brushed over them.

Her back bowed.

He cupped her breasts in his hands while his thumbs caressed her nipples.

Her eyelids closed as he continued his strokes before his hands moved slowly down the front of her torso and her hips. "You are a goddess, Lily."

She moaned as his hands glided over her thighs, pushing to widen them. The bed shifted and Lily opened her eyes to see Brandon prop his knee on the edge of the bed between her legs. He watched her face as his hands crept up her thighs where his fingertips glossed over her sex.

A single finger slid up the center of her, and she gripped the sheets, every nerve in her body alight with sensation. Her breathing shot to full capacity. She ached for release, to feel his touch on her. God, she even wanted him inside her. Lily never gave into one-night stands because it was just lust, no relationship. It would be meaningless. Tonight, for the first time, she was tempted to give in.

Brandon's muscles flexed and pushed against his shirt and pants, and his tanned skin peeked from the neckline. All she could imagine was how Brandon felt, how he looked naked, how he kissed.

He smoothed her liquid heat over her clit. "You are so wet, Lily," he said in awe. "I can't wait to see how beautiful you look when you come."

He braced his other hand on the bed while he continued his ministrations- caressing, circling her clit, and slowly pressing a finger inside. He worked so slowly, no sudden movements, as if to ensure he didn't frighten her. But God, she needed to come. Her face warmed with every passing second.

She spread her legs farther apart. *Please don't stop.*

He stroked his free hand over her thigh, her mons, her stomach, like he petted a kitten. Then he nearly took her breath away. He leaned down over her and slowly dragged his tongue through her center up to her clit.

"Ah," she cried out, stars dancing before her eyes.

He flattened his tongue to gently work her engorged clit, while his finger pushed back inside her.

"Brandon, *please* don't stop."

18

He groaned his response. His tongue pressed, adding pressure to her sensitive clit, while he slid another finger inside her. His fingers stroked in and pulled back all while his tongue made love to her sex.

The only sounds in the room were the slip-slide of his fingers inside her and the panting from her racing heart.

Lily loved when a man went down on her. *Especially* when that man knew what he was doing. Brandon knew *exactly* what he was doing. Her eyelids closed as she savored the sensations.

Her climax built from deep inside. Because Brandon moved so slowly, it rose to the surface the same way. Excruciatingly, deliciously slowly.

"Ahh."

And there was no stopping it. The orgasm grew to a maximum, roaring and sending energy to every inch of her body. She arched her neck and cried out his name, barely remembering her own, and panted, sucking in air.

Her body went limp. She opened her eyes to see Brandon studying her face, his eyes dark as the night sky.

His tongue swiped his lips clean. "Beautiful," he simply said.

He removed his fingers from her, then grabbed the blanket to cover her naked body. She lay stunned, staring up at him, and fascinated at how the best orgasm in her life was given to her by a perfect stranger.

He leaned down and kissed her forehead. "Thank you for sharing that with me, Lily. Sweet dreams," he whispered over her damp skin.

He reached for the lamp, switching off the light. She heard the rustle of his jacket and luggage, his footfalls, and the door open and close behind him.

She exhaled. "Holy fuck."

What the fuck! Brandon had no business touching Lily, claiming her like that. He couldn't resist. The lust that had consumed every cell in his body took over the sensible man. He was drawn to her in a way he'd never experienced before, as primal as male to female.

And God, how sweet she tasted. He'd had no intention of it going so far when he'd offered to "help" her. *Dammit!*

Assigned a new room, the hotel comped him a free meal at their restaurant to make amends. Whatever. He needed to get to his room, fast, before he scared everyone with his dick tenting his pants.

His room was a duplicate of Lily's. His sister had told him about the charming hotel, and how specialists were brought in for refurbishing to preserve the history. He was sure Leena was just trying to expose him to some culture. What's new, he thought with a smile.

After quickly getting settled, he blasted the shower on high, stripped naked, and jumped in. He'd taken himself in hand as lust coursed through his veins like an out-of-control wildfire. Women rarely caused such a reaction as Lily Bennett.

She was different. She was special. Her body was simply exquisite. Her smooth pale skin, the curve of her breasts and how her tapered waist fanned back out creating the perfect roundness of her hips. Her silhouette was extraordinary with clothes on, but completely naked? She was a goddess. A body built to satisfy a man's dreams.

Then to top it off, she was smart, witty, and had a great sense of humor. He could tell she took pride in her job and was likely highly competent. How remarkable that he ran into her again.

And she trusted him. He didn't know what he had done to deserve that trust, but he would do all he could to keep it.

Early the next morning, Brandon sent a note asking her to join him for dinner at the hotel's only restaurant. He'd meant it when he had invited her to dinner. And now because of what transpired the previous night, well, he had to see her again. Naked or not, it didn't really matter. He had to know more about her. And, any available time they had in Rome, he wanted to spend it with her.

Chapter 3

LILY FINISHED THE last of her makeup, tamping down the ridiculous smile from her face, when a knock came at the door. *It couldn't be.*

The flush warmed her cheeks instantly. She inhaled then raced for the door. The smiling, young bellhop decked in black and white carried a large bouquet of white roses.

"*Signorina* Bennett, these are for you. May I place them on the table?" He motioned to her small suite.

"*Si*. Of course." She quickly retrieved some bills from her wallet and tipped him. "*Grazie*."

"*Prego*," he said with a bow before leaving.

She turned and sniffed the beautiful roses. What a surprise! She lifted the card. As she suspected, the gift was from Brandon, inviting her to dinner at the hotel's restaurant for that evening.

Her body tingled at the delightful thought of seeing him again. She was crazy to even consider starting something when she had three nights left, but she couldn't help herself. She flattered herself into thinking he might be interested, even if it was just sex.

Truly, she wouldn't kid herself about the extent of what she meant to him. A man like Brandon could have *any* woman he wanted. She was a plaything, but she didn't give a hoot. Unlike the beginnings of her relationship with Kirk, her eyes were wide open. Not that this was a relationship, she chuckled softly because damn if this didn't feel empowering.

After Kirk, she deserved to be pampered, to be adored. Even if it was only for a few short days—and nights. That's right, damn it!

She dashed into the bathroom. Checked for any final touches, slipped on her sensible low-heeled shoes, grabbed her purse, and headed out to the wondrous city of Rome.

The taxi ride took her outside the city circle and east for about thirty minutes. There, the company had a few farms growing the ingredients for their skin care products—the rest were farther north in Tuscany.

That day she'd meet with Alberto. The last time she'd visited the plant a few modifications needed to be made. She felt confident the adjustments were made, but it was her job to ensure they were.

The following day, her tour was at ALK's newest facility near Siena where the company had acquired a rose farm. Rose hip was purportedly rich in antioxidants that ALK wanted to integrate into their lineup. The next day she'd witness the rose plants getting pollinated, but since it was early summer, she'd have to return in later summer and fall to see the plants in full bloom. She sighed, realizing that because of the buy-out, the likelihood of that was low.

If she were smart, though, she could plan some time in Siena after her tour. She'd heard so much about the small town.

She arrived at the factory and was immediately greeted by the plant manager—a short, slightly round man with graying hair and a smile that stretched from ear to ear.

"*Signorina* Lily. So good to see you," he nearly bounced to her and placed a kiss on each cheek.

"Alberto, good to see you." She kissed him back.

"Come see. We have just finished a batch of rich, creamy cleanser. You will love it!"

Of course she would, because Alberto loved it. He loved his job. He loved the products. And he made everyone else love them too.

Lifting her hand, he gently spread a dab of the cleanser on the back of her hand. "*Buona*, ah?"

"*Si*. Very smooth. Show me around, Alberto."

It was standard protocol. Lily was shown the factory with the huge steel cylinders holding product. Product traveled on the conveyor belt, and the workers in their white lab coats worked with plastic tubes and glass bottles. Everything appeared sterile and sanitary. Her job, in part, was to make sure things were as clean as they appeared.

Alberto stopped periodically and showed her the process for certain products coming down the line. He always had positive words for the product and the workers. She scanned the space, area by area, and made mental notes. Everything looked to be operating efficiently; Alberto was a good factory manager.

They walked to his office to review the work logs, errors, time schedules, output, a whole host of business minutiae. If she were new to this job, her head would be swimming, but she knew the facility like the back of her hand. She shuddered to think what the next person would do with it.

After lunch, she and Alberto visited several farms on the electric mule. The weather was clear, perfect for a tour. They made a few stops to investigate and discuss further.

Lily was anxious to get back to her hotel and make notes before dinner. And frankly, leave notes for whomever might inherit this position in the future. The busyness of the day had her too distracted to think about Brandon, but now that she had, he wouldn't budge from her mind.

The embarrassment from the previous night could easily overrun her, but she would not let her actions stop her from enjoying her short escapade with him. And she had just a few hours to shore up the reserves to see him again. He was handsome, smart, perhaps rich, and for some unknown reason had a thing for shapely women, namely her.

She took the cab back to the hotel, knowing tomorrow would be another long day, but all she cared about right then was seeing Brandon again.

She showered, layered on some exquisite, scented body lotion from the ALK collection, and slipped on a cotton dress with spaghetti straps and three-inch wedges. She stalled long enough—vacillating over whether or not to decline his offer. *Be brave.* After one last check of her lipstick, she grabbed her keycard and her wrap, and headed to the restaurant.

She breathed in several times and blew out through rounded lips. Her nerves were on edge. She'd let this man, this wonderfully talented and gorgeous man, do . . . things to her. How could she face him?

The elevator landed on the ground floor and she proceeded to the restaurant, passing the front desk, the coffee shop, and a gift shop. She identified herself to the hostess and was shown to Brandon's table. Her heart skipped a beat when she saw him rise from his chair. He wore a charcoal suit minus the tie. His dark eyes seared her, and the smile across his lips nearly had her breathless. *Gorgeous.*

Lily came into view at the hostess stand.

"I'll have to call you back," he said to his CFO on the phone.

Heels. She wore high heels that showed her shapely legs in the best possible way. He loved to see Lily in high heels. And her beautiful cleavage, the sway of her hips, her flowing dress, all had his mouth watering.

"Good evening," he said softly as he leaned down to kiss her cheek, filling his nostrils with her sweet scent.

She smiled, her cheeks a rose color. "Good evening."

He pulled back her chair and couldn't look away as her hand swept her skirt under her sexy ass.

"I'm so glad you could join me. You look lovely."

She glanced down briefly. "Thank you. And thank you for the beautiful flowers. You didn't have to do that."

The waiter interrupted, asking for their drink orders. "Do you like red wine, Lily?"

"Yes." A sweet smile graced her face.

He ordered a bottle of Masseto Toscana and several appetizers. Then turning back to his date, he said, "I know, but I wanted to. I very much enjoyed last night, but more importantly I wanted to see you again." The flowers reminded him of her white satin robe, but the petals were almost as silky as her skin.

She blushed and reached for a sip of water.

He leaned forward and grasped her free hand. "Please. I hope I didn't embarrass you. I would feel horrible if you regretted last night."

"It's just that we hardly know each other." Lily glanced down briefly as her chest rose and fell. "I don't regret it, Brandon. I liked it. A lot." Her blue eyes penetrated him.

He stroked a thumb over the back of her soft hand. Her pause made him think she wanted to say more, and the stain in her cheeks told him what it was.

Her thoughts matched his thoughts, his reaction. He could already feel his dick flex in his pants. He lifted her hand to his lips. "I am in town for a week. How long are you staying?"

"I, um, I'm staying four days, three more nights."

"Perhaps you have some time during your trip when we could see each other again?"

The corners of her pink lips lifted. "Yes, I do."

If he had his way, he would see her every day while she was there.

They toasted to the trip and sampled the hot hors d'oeuvres.

She went back to the conversation. "In fact, I need to go to Siena tomorrow. I'm on an early train, and I was thinking after work I would tour the town. Would you care to join me?"

He had a meeting that would take him until five in the afternoon, at the earliest. He'd rented a car so he could drive, but even still, Siena was over two hours away.

"It's okay. I know you're busy." She interrupted his thoughts with a wave of her hand.

Lily's face exhibited shyness, which confused him because she had to know he wanted to see her again.

"I'll meet you," he said definitively. "I have a car. You just tell me where and when, and I'll be there."

Brandon wasn't in the habit of juggling meetings, but in this case, he'd make an exception. He could not recall in all of his adult years ever meeting someone like her. He was not ready to let her go, knowing of course he had zero time for relationships.

Lily smiled. "Okay. But if something comes up, I understand. I'll give you my cell phone number."

She did it again, giving him a way out. Her reticence left him puzzled, so he'd make an effort to show her his interest.

They lounged over their dinner, chatting, drinking, laughing. She asked more about his parents, his sisters- Katie and Leena, and growing up in Florida. In turn, he learned about her parents and growing up an only child. She apparently had a close friend, Courtney, she referred to her as a "sister from another mister". She asked some of the most intriguing questions, like *Who has been the biggest influence in your life?* And *What's your favorite place in the whole world?* He enjoyed her company so much, he hadn't realized almost three hours had passed.

"It's gotten late, but would you like to walk for a bit?"

"That would be great." Her eyes twinkled at him.

They stepped outside the restaurant and she lifted her wrap off her arm.

"Here. Let me help you."

"Thank you."

He raised the soft fabric to her bare shoulders and let his fingertips glaze over her skin a moment longer. She shivered and he smiled, loving how she responded to his touch.

He didn't wait for an invitation, but took her hand and walked with her along the sidewalk in the more quiet part of Rome. Night fell and open shops and street lamps lit the way.

They passed old stone buildings, and in several places, the sidewalks were stone as well. Lily had no problem navigating them in her heels. Some streets were busier with locals and tourists. Most of the areas though were quiet with very few cars. He smiled at her, and noticed how golden brown her hair looked in the moonlight.

A ping hit Brandon hard.

All he wanted was to have his lips on her. In fact, he was distracted today thinking about her. Kissing a woman like Lily, anywhere on Lily, would be a dream come true.

He gave in. With a slight tug of her hand, he led her to an alcove in front of a closed store. She glanced up at him, questioning.

"Lily, I've wanted to do one thing all night."

"Okay?"

"I want to kiss you."

She stared at him and her full mouth curved upward. His hand cupped her jaw and a thumb smoothed over her bottom lip.

He lowered his head, gently touching his lips to hers. One taste and he wanted more. His hands cupped her nape to take the kiss deeper, sliding his tongue against hers. A small moan escaped her precious mouth. He sought her, craved her kiss, and she returned it with the same eagerness.

He pressed her against the glass door, knowing she would feel his growing erection. Her arms looped around his neck. He let one hand slide down her soft neck and trace the outside of her breast. She mewled, and that spurred him on.

His lips traveled down her neck as his hand cupped her breast. "I love your breasts," he whispered over her lips. He drew a thumb across her nipple, and she arched into his touch.

"Yes," she breathed.

Her hands slid down his neck and shoulders to his chest. She pushed open his jacket and caressed his chest. He craved her hands on him. She slid further south and he didn't stop her.

His stiff cock ached for more, his balls grew heavy. He could only think about her, lying naked on her hotel bed, waiting for him to dive into her.

"Brandon, I want to touch you," she breathed against his mouth.

He pulled back to meet her eyes. Blue eyes that could look right through him.

They were in a public place, and although it was dark and he had them tucked away, it was still incredibly risky. He wasn't a goddamn teenager. He was the president and CEO of a major corporation, acquiring an Italian business. What was he thinking?

And she actually knew people in that country. Gee-zus!

Who are you, she thought to herself. She worked her bottom lip. She'd just told a gorgeous man, a practical stranger, that she wanted to touch him. Her fingers itched to feel his soft skin, to wrap her hand around his warm cock, to smooth pre-cum over his swollen head. Her heart played staccato in her chest, and her sex was slick.

Her shaky hands slipped passed his waistband to his firm cock, pressing on the fine fabric of his pants. She stroked a hand up and down. His breath quickened.

One peek over his shoulder at the quiet street behind them, she returned to his gaze as she searched for the tab of his fly. His eyes widened, but he didn't stop her.

"Lily."

She pleaded with her eyes while she slowly drew down his zipper.

She was crazy, she knew it. But if she only lived once, she would take a chance. A chance with a man she would never see again after this trip.

Another glance behind him, and her fingers smoothed over his underwear. She tucked her hand through the placket of his briefs and as she took a hold of him, he moaned into her hair.

She stroked with one hand, and pushed the fabric aside with the other hand, letting him free, careful to shield them from any possible foot traffic.

"Fuck, Lily," he growled.

She gripped him, loving his soft skin. His size allowed her to use two hands. He felt so incredible-bigger than her vibrator, bigger than Kirk.

"I want you to come, Brandon."

He grunted, and his pelvis flexed slightly.

The power she had over him right then was heady. This sexy man would come at her touch, and she would savor every moment.

"Lily. If you don't stop, I'll make a mess."

Her teeth bit the inside of her cheek. She hadn't thought this through. All she wanted was to have her hands on him, to bring him pleasure. She pulled the wrap off her shoulders.

"I'll take care of it, Brandon." She smoothed the pre-cum with her thumb.

"Christ, sweetheart. You're killing me. You feel so good, I don't want you to stop."

He slammed one hand on the glass door to brace himself, and with the other, he cupped her face and crashed his lips to hers—his kiss voracious.

Short moments later, he slid his cheek against her face and stifled his groan in her hair. He growled and she felt the hot semen in her hands as she continued to fist him. He flexed twice more as the last drops came out.

With her wrap, she wiped him gingerly, and then her hands. He breathed heavily.

"Fuck, that was amazing."

She carefully put him back together and closed his pants. She smiled inside. The elation had her feeling like the goddess he called her the prior night.

He inched backward, his eyes glazed. "Lily, that was the craziest thing I've ever done."

"Ha," burst from her mouth. "Well, I suppose now you know what last night felt like for me then."

He grinned, showing his beautiful white teeth. "Touché."

He tapped his finger on her wrap. "Will that come clean?"

"It should." *And if it doesn't, it was worth every blessed penny.*

He nodded. "C'mon. You have an early morning, and I don't want you tired tomorrow night."

She looked up at him with a raised brow. He was already planning tomorrow night?

At the door of her hotel room, he kissed her deeply and stroked a hand down the side of her arm. "Lily, you're incredible," he said close to her face. "Good night."

"Good night." She pulled her keycard out of pocket, and after one last glance at him, she ducked inside.

She gently closed the door, and leaned back against it, and exhaled. She shook her head and wondered where the reserved, sometimes self-conscious girl had gone.

Chapter 4

BRANDON LISTENED TO the CFO of the mid-sized Italian company review the litany of financials, most of which he already knew. The room was filled with smart men and women eager for the acquisition, the largest in Laurel's history, to take place.

The day for Brandon was packed with meeting upon meeting, all part of the due diligence to make sure the sale happened without a hitch. One more to go and he would be on his way to Lily.

Her scent wafted from this shirt from their encounter the previous night. She intoxicated him. He'd actually considered seeing her when they returned to the States, but how could that happen when he currently resided in Miami and she in Los Angeles? Not to mention he had zero time for a relationship. Laurel Med was thrust upon him unexpectedly; he could not let his family, the board, or the shareholders down.

"Brandon?" Franco Serra asked.

Brandon sat a large conference room table surrounded by chairs, every one filled with Corticelli Lab executives including Gian Esposito, their CEO, and Franco Serra, their CFO. Everything from the whiteboard to the notepads looked very much like any average American room setting, except in place of a pitcher of coffee sat an espresso machine.

"Yes, sorry." *Shit*. Being caught daydreaming did not make a good impression on the people looking to trust you with their future.

"I asked about job loss. Do you have an idea of how many people you will put out of work?"

"We anticipate no job losses, just restructuring in a few areas."

Several eyebrows went up.

Brandon leaned forward, rested his forearms on the conference room table and inhaled. "Folks, you have a solid company here. There are duplicate products that Laurel sells, but you are also in areas we were looking to expand, such as nanotechnology. Not to mention your presence in Europe. If things go as I expect they will, we will need to *increase* headcount."

"That's good news," said Gian, who would soon be retired on a handsome severance package.

Finally, Brandon's last meeting dealt with a lot of the legal and tax regulations involved in buying a foreign company. He had his top two attorneys with him to get a thorough understanding of what the Italian government expected from a US company in situations such as this.

"Before we sign anything, is this an inversion?" Corticelli's lead attorney, Lorenzo Rossi, spoke in a gravelly voice, a scowl on his face. The older gentleman with the large belly and a Roman nose looked to be one bad day away from a coronary.

Brandon sat back at the abrupt question. The man seemed concerned with an inversion that meant reincorporation in a foreign country. From the corner of his eye, Brandon noticed one of his lawyers glance his way.

"Why do you ask?" Brandon controlled his facial expression, keeping it neutral.

The attorney crossed his arms. "We understand you are moving your headquarters."

He hid his surprise. The fact that Laurel was moving its headquarters wasn't yet public knowledge. And why the hell would the man even care?

Brandon couldn't fathom what a logistical nightmare moving corporate headquarters to Italy would be. Unless . . . Rossi was just flexing his legal muscle, letting everyone in the room know he was savvy on the ways American corporations avoided taxes.

Well, that simply wasn't the way Brandon chose to run his business.

"Yes, that's true; however headquarters will remain in the US. This acquisition offers Laurel a European base. And we see excellent synergy between the two companies. This is not for an inversion."

The man studied Brandon for what seemed like an eternity. What the hell was his problem? If he wanted to go toe to toe, Brandon would welcome it. In fact, he'd check his civility at the door, if necessary.

"Alright," the attorney finally said.

The rest of the meeting proceeded without issue. Brandon glanced at his phone, not that he'd expected a text from Lily. When he knew the meat of the discussion was done, he made his excuses and departed early, leaving his legal eagles to finish up. He was already exhausted and this was only day two. Five more to go. He had one thing on his mind, and he didn't want to delay another moment in getting to Lily and her lush, warm body. And he had a plan. If all went well, Brandon would have her in his bed that night.

Brandon brought the dream of a sports car to a slow stop in front of the farm's small house which had been converted to offices. His phone rang— another business call—he couldn't ignore. He wrapped the call as quickly as possible so he could get to Lily.

He entered the building, and seeing no one to greet him, he followed the sound of voices down a hall.

Lily stood before a gentleman who was dressed in blue jeans, discussing something about fertilizer and timing of harvest while leaning over a schematic spread out in front of them. They didn't notice Brandon at the door. The man responded, and she nodded and quickly followed up with another question. Brandon knew little of what was said, but drew his attention to how Lily handled herself. He stared in awe. She mirrored the man's body language, smiled when warranted, and spoke intelligently with the Italian.

He watched her in action, and he was impressed. In fact, it made him hard. He cleared his throat.

"Oh, Brandon. I didn't hear you," Lily said, turning toward the door, her eyes smiling.

"Sorry to interrupt. No one was at the front desk." He reached a hand to the Italian. "Hello, I'm Brandon."

"Hello. Damarco." He turned to look at Lily. "We are done here, yes?"

Lily nodded. "I'll get my things. Thanks for everything, Damarco."

"*Si, signorina.*" Damarco shook her hand, cupping it.

Instinctively, Brandon laid his hand on Lily's lower back, guiding her to the car. Work was finally done for the day, and it was time for the two of them.

Lily's day couldn't have gone better. The new farm she'd toured had lived up to her expectations and would be fruitful in the coming months. The maintenance and management of the farm met the standards that ALK demanded. This happiness also held sorrow because she'd never see the true potential of what the land could produce.

Instead she focused her attention on the man next to her, holding her hand, his other hand on the steering wheel of a sleek red Italian sports car.

His Prada aviator sunglasses, luxurious, tailored cotton shirt, and chiseled jawline made him look every bit a powerful executive. And why he wanted to spend time her, still baffled her.

"You're lost in thought."

She turned his way. "Sorry, thinking about work," she lied. Confessing that she'd been thinking about him, about them, wouldn't be wise.

"Was it a rough day?"

"Not really. The farm is good. Very good really. Everything my company expects." She settled into her seat.

"So, where's the problem?"

"No problem," she half-smiled. "Just lots to do."

"Your company is very serious about this rose hip farm." It wasn't a question.

He briefly glanced her way before returning his attention to the winding road. He seemed interested in her job, not just making conversation.

"Yes, as I mentioned they have strict requirements to be as natural and organic as possible. They depend on me to be the eyes and ears for them." Her shoulders slumped just thinking about the looming loss of her job.

"That's a lot of responsibility."

She hadn't thought about it that way, but he was correct. Lily took pride in her job. Knowing she might not be there in the future—checking on the progress, making sure standards were met—made her stomach twist. This job was no run-of-the-mill job. The entire reason for having the product made overseas was to maintain the high level of purity and quality.

She nodded. "It is."

"You seem incredibly competent at your job."

Warmth spread across her cheeks. "I guess so."

He merely smiled.

"So, enough about me. How was your day? And where are we going?" Maybe she could search him later on the Internet.

They'd been traveling for a while, and drove through the heart of Siena. She furrowed her brows. If he planned on taking her out to eat, being in town might be their best option.

"Well, to answer your second question. We're going to dinner. I heard of a quiet little place, just north of town, where we can dine overlooking the sunset."

Seriously? "The sunset? That sounds incredible."

He gave a little squeeze of her fingers. "Doesn't it? Then maybe we can walk through town. Then . . ." he lifted her hand and kissed the back of it, which instantly awakened her. Not that it took much effort on Brandon's part to bring her body alive. Being with Brandon made Kirk a distant memory. "I'd like us to check in to a hotel and stay the night—together."

Just hearing the silky words fall from his lips set her nerves on fire. She swallowed. "You want to spend the night in Siena? I don't have a toothbrush or anything."

He kissed her knuckles. "Don't worry about that. Because yes, I want to spend the night with you, Lily. I want to strip you down and explore every inch of your body. I want to learn what pleases you," his voice dropped to a deep rich timbre, "and I want to please you over and over again."

Her insides liquefied. She licked her dry lips and all she could muster was a simple nod of her head.

His cell phone vibrated on the table. He lifted it, glanced at the screen and silenced the thing.

"You can take that, if you need to," she said almost apologetically.

"No. It will keep."

A feeling of guilt washed over her. He had a merger to facilitate and instead he was wasting his valuable time, spending it with her.

"What are you thinking?" he broke her train of thought.

"That you work very hard."

He nodded, thoughtful. "I do. My father had a heart attack, and was forced to resign early. So I've had to take on more. I, like you, love what I do, but times like this, work gets in the way. Whoever is trying to get a hold of me can wait until morning," he gave her a reassuring smile.

"Now how about dessert?"

He wrapped an arm around her shoulders to watch the sunset and fed her bites of chocolate cake.

"Incredible." The chocolate was rich, but not overly sweet. The smooth texture practically melted in her mouth.

"Mmmhmm," he murmured after slipping in a bite. "But I'm sure it won't be the only delicious thing I taste tonight," he said low in her ear.

The blood rushed to her face, sending color anew to her cheeks.

"I think I'd like that," she whispered.

He leaned forward, raising her chin with his finger, and aligning his lips over hers. His kiss started slowly, testing, and as her lips parted his smooth tongue danced with hers. His warm hand cupped her jaw and her body relaxed into his. He brought his head back to meet her gaze just as she opened her eyes.

"More later," he said with a soft smile.

She managed to make it through dinner, knowing the flush in her cheeks hadn't subsided. Brandon spoke about his company, his family, the acquisition, and she was mesmerized by him. Mesmerized by the way his lips moved, the subtle expression in his eyes, and his magnetic smile. He could have *any* woman he pleased, and he chose to be with her.

"Let's go walk through town," he suggested after dinner.

Brandon wove his fingers through hers. The warmth in his hand was both calming and exhilarating. Lily's heart skipped a beat, and she allowed herself to be transported into the fantasy where they were boyfriend/girlfriend strolling through the very charming ancient town of Siena. That she meant the world to him, and he for her.

They strolled through the narrow streets, admiring the stone buildings with garden window boxes, slowly making their way to a café at the city center. They each sipped on cappuccino, marveling over Siena's bi-annual horse race that took place right where they sat.

"Is there anything else you wanted to see while you were here, Lily?"

The heart of Tuscany was beautiful, all she had imagined it would be. She breathed in the night air. This trip to Italy quickly grew from something she'd dreaded into something beyond her wildest dreams. She turned his way, hypnotized by the glimmer in his eyes. Her time with Brandon would be short, so she had only one reply. "No. I think I'd like to go to the hotel."

The spark in his eyes caused his entire face to shine. "Very well then."

He rose and held open a hand for her. She took it, feeling the instant warmth travel up her arm. She didn't know exactly what the evening held, but the hours of anticipation were soon coming to an end.

Instead of returning to his car, they walked several blocks to a quaint hotel called Santa Cristina. Softly glowing lights and small balconies at every room welcomed them. Brandon checked in, and Lily could only smile at his broken Italian. *So, there is one thing he's not very good at.*

Then, he grabbed her hand and led her to the hotel's gift shop.

He briskly stalked through the shop pulling toiletries—a toothbrush, toothpaste, deodorant—off the shelf, placing them on the counter.

"Follow me."

This determined and focused side of Brandon Lily hadn't seen before. She bit the inside of her cheek and did as he bid. He stopped in front of a rack of women's clothing, a few high-end labels she recognized.

"Brandon, I don't need any of this," she implored. "I can rinse my underwear in the sink."

"Of course you do." He examined a deep blue sheath dress and held it in front of her. It was gorgeous. She reached out. *Holy crap*! The nubby fabric felt like silk.

"Please. I don't mind wearing these clothes in the morning."

He hung the dress on the rack and pivoted toward her. Lifting her chin to meet his fiery gaze, he moved closer. "There is no way I will allow you to do a walk of shame tomorrow. I'm not giving you any reason to regret tonight."

He looped an arm around her waist and pulled her to him. Her hands landed against his chest for balance. "And the way I'm feeling right now, there is a high probability that I will rip those clothes off your delectable body before I fuck you into next month."

She swallowed hard. No one had ever spoken to her in such a way. Lust flooded her body, the feel of his erection pressed against her caused her sex to ache. Right then, she wanted Brandon more than she had ever wanted a man before.

She opened her mouth, but no words came out.

Brandon grinned, and kissed her cheek softly. "Now please go over there and pick out a bra and panties, and any cosmetics you might need."

She did as he instructed, finding something black and lacy, and met him at the sales counter. Lily honed in on *two* dresses the sales lady wrapped up, but she knew better than to argue. Brandon laid down a platinum credit card, but strangely added nothing to the pile for himself.

With the dresses protected under plastic and everything else nestled in a shopping bag, Brandon motioned for them to leave. Moments later, they exited the elevator for the top floor and stopped in front of a door at the end of the hall.

Lily quietly took in a deep breath and wondered if she was living out a dream or making a deal with the devil.

Chapter 5

BRANDON UNLOCKED THE door and held it open for Lily to enter. The hotel suite was luxurious, spacious, and exactly what he wanted when he'd booked it.

He rested the shopping bag on the nearest table and moved to the bedroom to hang Lily's dresses in the closet. His dick was so fucking hard he didn't know how he wanted to take her first. He had that night and the next with Lily, and then she'd be flying back to the States. He didn't want to waste a single moment.

He returned to the main room to find her looking out the French doors into the night. The entire suite was done in an appealing gray-blue and white, with dark brown furniture. And the large king bed had already been turned down. Despite the opulent and comfortable surroundings, all Brandon could focus on was Lily. He'd love to strip her down naked, take her out to the balcony, and be inside her in sixty seconds flat. He inhaled deeply through his nostrils.

Stopping behind her, he laid his hands at her hips.

"This place is amazing," she said softly as she turned to face him.

He placed a small kiss on her temple. For their first time together, he would need to maintain control. He could not just jump on her.

"Would you like something to drink?"

"Perhaps some water."

He retrieved two bottled waters from the fridge, opened one, and handed it to her. She watched him, even as she drank. She might be hesitant, but he knew the passion Lily had deep inside. And his eagerness to let it out had his pulse racing.

"Thank you. And thank you for the dresses. You didn't have to do that."

He closed the space between them and placed her water next to his. "I wanted to." He scraped his lips over hers gently. "Lily, I want to know something."

Her eyes narrowed. "Okay."

He pulled back to meet her gaze but held on to her hips. "Tell me about your ex."

Her chin lowered, and she looked so fucking adorable the way she stared at him. She tried to step back, but he kept her in place.

"What do you want to know?"

"What was his name?"

"Kirk."

"How long were you two together?" His thumbs made small circles at her hips.

"Almost three years."

"Did he make you happy?"

Her eyes glanced down briefly. "At first, yes. But as time passed, things changed. I guess we grew apart."

"I see. Did he make you happy in bed?"

He heard the quick rush of air as she gasped. He held her gaze, moving his thumbs in bigger circles against her skirt.

"Um, I guess."

He tugged her blouse out of her skirt waistband, and skimmed his thumbs over her warm silky skin.

"What are some things you two would do?"

She licked her pink lips. "Um, what do you mean?"

He worked his way to her blouse buttons and, starting from the bottom, began releasing them one by one. "Well, did he give you oral sex? Or you him?"

She glanced down at his hands briefly and nodded.

"Did he make you come when you two had sex?"

Brandon slipped her blouse off her shoulders, letting it fall to the floor.

She didn't answer the question, so he waited. He wanted to know, had to know, what the ex had given her. He knew he would be better, that wasn't a question. Fucking a woman like Lily would be euphoric for any man. The fact that the asshole couldn't keep her told Brandon he didn't measure up. And that he truly hadn't satisfied her.

He would release her sexuality that night, and take to her to heights she'd never before reached. He knew it, and he needed her to know it.

"Lily?"

"No. No, I didn't come when we had sex unless I used my vibrator."

Ah, yes. Seeing that vibrator by Lily's hotel bed would be an image he would hold forever.

"Turn around."

She presented her back to him and he unzipped her skirt, pushing it to the floor.

Her breathing increased.

"Step out."

As she kicked aside her skirt, he tugged the drapes closed.

She faced him again, her back to the closed draperies. She was exquisite. He grazed his hands over her creamy smooth skin, feeling every curve. His cock ached to be inside her.

Soon.

"Did he ever kiss your entire body from head to toe?"

He unfastened the buttons from his shirt and tossed the garment to the nearest piece of furniture.

She shook her head.

"You know, I love to have my lips all over you, Lily."

She smiled, and the pink in her cheeks matched her delicate bra and panties. He could smell her arousal and the need to taste her became overpowering.

He placed his hands on her cheeks and lowered his lips to hers. She opened and welcomed him, her tongue dancing with his. She held on to his shoulders and pressed her body closer. His hand slid around her back and unclipped her bra. He grabbed it and flung it aside.

"Fuck, I love your breasts." And immediately, cupping his hands around each breast, he sucked a nipple into his mouth. Her fingers dug into his shoulders and she arched her back, begging his mouth for more. He would pleasure her for as long as he could stand it before diving into her. The need could about kill him.

Be gentle the first time, he reminded himself.

He lowered himself to his knees before her, inhaling deeply. His hands stroked up and down her legs, cupping her delicious ass. "Lily, did your ex ever fuck you up against a wall?"

Her eyes went wide. But after only a beat, she shook her head.

"Place your hands on the wall behind you."

It may be a glass door, but it wasn't going anywhere. She did as he asked.

His two fingers hooked around her panties, and he slowly dragged them to the floor. Then he pulled off her shoes. Her gorgeous naked body stood before him. She was a modern-day Marilyn Monroe and that night he was the luckiest bastard to be with her.

With an easy motion of his tongue, Brandon slid through her wet slit. She moaned. He smoothed his hands over her thighs to her core and separated her lips. His tongue dove into her.

"Oh, God," she whimpered and widened her legs.

Her fingers wove through his hair as he toyed with her clit, pressing and lapping as much as she would take. Slight tremors started at her legs. He reached into his back pocket for a condom while circling her clit with his free hand. He undid his belt and covered himself in record time. He returned his eager mouth to her fruit and licked her intently.

"Oh," she moaned again.

He moved his tongue a little faster and slipped two fingers into her core. The tremors came on stronger and Lily's head fell against the wall as she moaned through her closed mouth. Her muscles contracted and tugged on him as her climax gave way.

After she mostly subsided, he rose, his pants falling to his ankles. He wrapped one arm around her waist and the other hand brought her leg up to his hip.

He reached under her thigh for her pussy, then lining up his cock, he dove into her as he lifted her at the same time.

She cried out.

"That's it. That's my girl," he growled. "Don't hold back. I want to hear you."

She nodded quickly, her mouth gaping to take in air. He held her flat against the wall and pumped into her warm body. The pink in her cheeks gave her face the most beautiful glow.

He pinned her body with his, covering his mouth over hers, and groaned when her full breasts crushed his bare chest. He thrust, her arms and legs wrapped tightly around him, they moved as one.

"Fuck, Lily. You feel amazing," he panted.

"Brandon."

He didn't know how long he could last; it might not be enough time for her to come again. But the night is still young, he thought.

He pumped harder and released the most explosive orgasm he'd ever had.

They remained there, pinned against the wall for several moments, recuperating from the exertion.

Holding her close, he walked her to the bathroom. He placed her on the floor mat so he could turn the shower on full force. He missed being inside her but his cock already started building a second wind.

"I want to wash you," he persuaded.

"Okay," she spoke in a soft tone with her eyes slightly glassy, as if still on an orgasmic high.

"And I'll try not to get your hair wet." Her shoulder-length hair tangled between his fingers perfectly just as it was.

She smiled at him.

He helped her into the shower, and soaked a washcloth in the spray.

She watched him load shower gel on the cloth, but her silence led him to believe she was thinking about something else.

"Brandon?"

"Yes?" He gently soaped her arms, one at a time.

"I don't believe you're married, but do you have a girlfriend back in the States?"

For the first time in a long time, Brandon fell speechless. He should have expected the question, but he somehow thought she'd understood.

Brandon had no room in his life for a woman—a relationship—not with running a company the size of Laurel. He never saw himself married, never planned on it. As it was, this escapade would cost him. He *had* planned to work every evening; now he was spending his nights with the beautiful, luscious Lily. Not that he regretted it. Not in the least. Time with Lily was hands-down the best time he'd spent with a woman, ever.

That's why what he and Lily had was so fucking perfect. It was just sex. Temporary and hot. He knew it. Lily knew it.

"No, Lily. I thought you knew. I am not married, never have been. Nor am I seeing anyone. I'm your typical workaholic. Work will always come first for me." He rinsed her arm under the spray.

When Lily's mind trailed back to their earlier conversation, and Brandon's questions about her ex, it brought up curiosity about his romantic involvements.

Asking him put her mind at ease-she believed him that he had no one waiting for him back home. Lily had to know for sure because she didn't sleep with married men, and the thought of him having someone in his life, well . . .

She nodded. "Okay."

"Anything else you want to know about me?" he asked.

She felt heat race across her face. "No. I should have asked earlier, but . . ."

He lifted her chin with his index finger. "You don't need to explain. I completely understand. Although this is temporary, you had to know if I was cheating on someone else with you."

Her cheeks grew warmer, and suddenly being naked in the shower became uncomfortable. Her arms crossed in front of her torso. "No, that's not it."

He kept his eyes trained on hers. "Sure, it is. But I don't stray. When I am with a woman, I'm seeing no one else." He leaned down for a quick peck on the lips. "And I love the way your face flushes when you're embarrassed."

God! She felt it again. "It's one of my worst traits."

"I think it's one of your best." He kissed her lips, longer this time. He pulled back a few inches, his eyes dark. "Now, how about we finish our shower."

She smiled. She realized Brandon wouldn't want to be naked long without making something good of it.

When he smiled back, she nearly melted. "Turn around, hands on the wall," he said. "I owe you an orgasm."

She did as he bid, the water spraying the sides of their bodies. He squirted more gel on the cloth and reached around to stroke it across her stomach. His hand made wide circles before sliding upward to her breasts.

His body connected with hers, his erection pressed firmly against her low back. He released the cloth and caressed her breasts with both hands, playing with her hardened nipples.

She moaned loudly and let her head drop backward on his shoulder. She closed her eyes, enjoying the pressure building at her sex.

"I could do this all day, Lily. And damn, I wish I had a condom in here." He lowered his hand to her sex. "Spread your legs wider."

She happily complied, and his finger dipped into her cleft and up and around her clit. "Oh, God," she breathed.

He tormented her slowly with his fingers, spreading her slickness around. "You feel so fucking good. I can't wait anymore."

He withdrew his hand and reached to shut off the water. "Come." He grabbed her hand and pushed the glass door open. Yanking the towel off the towel bar, he loosely wrapped her and continued to the bedroom. He left her by the bed, then briskly walked to a leather bag on the chair in the corner.

How had she missed that?

He wasted no time retrieving a condom and sheathing himself. She refused to turn her eyes away from his impressive erection. He strode to her and cupped the sides of her head, sealing his mouth to hers. Lust seemed to flow from every pore of his body, and it only fueled her. She let the towel fall and pressed herself to his wonderfully hard, naked body, clutching his strong shoulders. Her sex grew slicker with every passing moment.

He broke the kiss. "Hands on the bed, beautiful."

She pivoted her body and rested her hands on the bed. She didn't usually like this position because everything just hung down, unattractively, she might add. But with Brandon, and oh, his hands caressing her ass, she couldn't care less.

"Lily, you are going to come again. You'll come every time I fuck you."

His dirty talk was erotic. She never thought she'd like to hear that, but now she couldn't get enough.

He slid his hands lower, separating her as he pressed his glorious cock into her.

"Oh . . . Brandon," she panted.

Her head fell forward as she savored his slow entry. He kissed her back, licking droplets of water as he moved methodically in her. The walls of her pussy were alive with sensation, eager for more.

"You feel so good pulling on my cock, Lily." His hands cupped her breasts, and toying with her nipples heightened her arousal. "You will see fireworks when you come, but you won't touch your clit. Understand?"

She thought the last episode when he had her up against the glass was pretty phenomenal. He wanted to make her come during sex. And something inside her warmed at the notion. No other man before seemed as concerned about whether she'd came or not.

"Okay," she breathed.

And damn if she didn't think he was going to do it. The pressure at her pussy climbed quickly and steadily to where she hovered on a glorious plateau of pleasure.

"Oh, God, Brandon."

"Yes, beautiful." He maintained his pumping all while caressing her back, thighs, and breasts. He nibbled at her neck and shoulders. She was delirious with desire.

"Brandon. I need to come."

"You will." He increased speed, thrusting in and out, and pinched her nipples, the sting shooting straight to her sex.

"Ah!" Her climax gathered momentum from deep inside. He knew exactly what he was doing and she loved it. She panted, gripped the sheets when the euphoric explosion hit her full force. She cried out again.

She collapsed to the bed, her ears ringing from the joyous release.

Brandon followed her down, pushing her legs apart. "You are so beautiful when you come." He pushed back inside her, and instantly she clenched his cock. He filled her so completely.

Lily never knew sex could be like this. Kirk had nothing on Brandon. Brandon treated her like she was beautiful and sexy, like he couldn't get enough. Lily knew in her head this fling couldn't last, but she began to doubt that her heart was listening.

They dozed and slept like the dead. It had to be the best sleep of her entire life. Early in the morning, Brandon's lips and hands roamed her body, awaking her slowly. He whispered, *I'm sorry. I'm sorry. I need to be inside you again.*

"It's okay," she mumbled.

His hands trailed to her sex. "God, Lily. You're already wet."

Brandon did that to her. Her hormones were on overdrive around him. His touch, his kisses, his smile, his compliments—all made her feel wanted and cherished.

He laid her on her back, spread her legs apart, and to her delight, brought his talented mouth to her pussy. She sighed.

It took no time at all for him to bring her to orgasm. Then coming upright, he slowly pushed his sheathed cock inside her and crashed his mouth to hers. She could taste herself on him. So many erotic things that she would remember until her last breath.

She wrapped her legs and arms around him and focused on how he made love to her, how he made her feel. This was her last day in Italy. The following morning she'd need to return to the States. Return to no boyfriend, possibly no job, an empty apartment, and no more amazing sex. She forced her thoughts to stay with her and Brandon, making each other feel good. For as long as they could.

Chapter 6

BRANDON INTENTIONALLY CLEARED his calendar for the following morning so that his first appointment wouldn't happen until lunch. That gave him more time with Lily, and a chance for them to drive back to Rome together, unrushed. And fuck, he'd loved waking up with her naked body next to him.

After Brandon dropped Lily at a farm just outside Rome, he drove to his appointment. He expected a leisurely sort of lunch, CEO to CEO. A chance to bid the old CEO farewell and toast his upcoming retirement. Instead, the hostess showed Brandon to the table. And no small surprise, next to the CEO of Corticelli was the attorney from yesterday, Lorenzo Rossi. The knot grew in his stomach because he knew this could go one of two ways—happy to make friends with the new "boss" or here to stir up trouble again.

Gian and Lorenzo were seated on one side of a rectangular table. Brandon took an available seat across the table, placed the linen napkin on his lap, and exchanged pleasantries while his water glass was filled. He patiently waited to hear what was on Lorenzo's mind.

"Mr. Morgan, I wanted to bring this up again, without an audience. Everyone is rather uneasy about this acquisition."

Everyone or you?

"We're not sure if you're really thinking about an inversion but our most crucial concern is jobs. You say there will be no job loss. But usually situations like this don't bode well for the purchased company."

Brandon couldn't tell if the attorney was sincerely nervous about the acquisition, or if he was just stirring up trouble. Over Brandon's dead body would he let *this suit* stop the acquisition, all so he could look after his own self-interests. This merger would be good for both companies, it would be good for the healthcare industry. And with an aging population, it would be good for the world as a whole.

Gian wore a faint expression of disbelief. Brandon caught a subtle shake of the CEO's head, as if he couldn't believe Lorenzo continued to press the issue.

Brandon tried a different approach. A direct, American-style approach. "As I see it, the only job at risk is yours."

Lorenzo's eyes flew open. Gian looked up from his appetizer, glancing at each man. Brandon let the corners of his lips curve upward, and soon Gian released a belly laugh that grew deeper and deeper each passing moment.

Brandon chuckled aloud and enjoyed his own personal triumph. "Lorenzo, know that the reason I am buying your company is because of how it functions *now*. As this trip has proved to me, you have done an outstanding job of building a solid company. Not to mention, there will be great synergy between our companies. Stop worrying so much. Let's enjoy a delicious meal together."

Gian looked at his attorney, and nodded. "He's right."

And bless the angels above, the rest of the meal continued without incident.

Brandon wanted this acquisition to go through more than he wanted anything else in his life. Not only would it be good for Laurel, but he'd prove to Wall Street and to his family that he could handle it. He would not fail. After all the months of due diligence, this acquisition was as good as done. Not Gian, nor Lorenzo, nor anyone else would stand in the way of this deal going through.

But rest assured, if Lorenzo brought up the topic one more time, Brandon would make his proclamation come true.

***

Lily's last day in Rome contained many meetings, long but necessary. For a woman about to be laid off, she shouldn't care so much, but she did. Her heart ached for the loss of the job, *and* for the final night she would have with Brandon.

He knocked at her hotel room door to take her to dinner. He wore a suit as usual, tailored to fit him like a second skin, showing off his strong shoulders, firm chest, and trim waist.

This night, he was all hers. And if this was to be her last night living an incredible fantasy, she would give it her all. *Be brave.*

So instead of being prepared for dinner, she'd prepped for Brandon. The door swung open and she invited him in.

His eyes traveled up and down her body, no doubt confused by the white robe she wore.

"Lily, are you not feeling well?"

"I feel fine. Are you hungry?" She sauntered to the table and poured him a glass of wine.

"A bit. Are you?" His head tipped slightly.

"Yes." She took a sip and put her glass down. "But not for food, just yet." With those words, she loosened the sash of her robe and pushed it to the floor, revealing her scantily-clothed body to Brandon.

Her first full day, when the taxi had taken her to the farm outside of the city, her eye caught a tiny lingerie shop around the corner from the hotel. With just a few minutes to spare, she raced there after her last meeting and fell in love. The sales woman showed her *the most* exquisite array of satin and lacy underthings.

The sales woman gushed. *Oh, you must try on this red set. Your man will love it.* And *If you don't have a fabulous black satin corset, you must try this one. Your bosom will look positively perfect.* She must have brought fifteen different ensembles into the dressing room, and actually helping Lily out of her clothes, dressed her in the finery. Lily loved being pampered and admired how she looked because she knew Brandon would love it too. She bought six different outfits, hoping to decide on one for their last night together.

She heard the sharp intake of air, and she stepped closer to him. "I would like *you* for an appetizer."

His smile grew as his gaze roamed her body from head to toe. "Whatever the lady wants."

She took his glass and set it next to hers, then proceeded to methodically strip her virile man. Her hands moved slowly, feeling every angle and ripple of his body, until he was left wearing only his boxer briefs.

She grazed her fingers up his strong arms to his chest, stopping at his jaw. She raised herself onto her toes and pressed her body against his for a kiss. He tasted of wine and mint.

His hands skimmed up her arms, over her shoulders, and trailed the outline of her red lace bra. "I love this on you," he breathed over her lips.

"I'd hoped you would."

Her fingers trailed down his abdomen toward his swollen erection. He growled when her hands cupped him through the fabric. In one single movement, she lowered herself to her knees, taking his underwear to the ground. His cock sprung free, inches from her mouth.

She wanted to taste him. There he stood and the desire to have him in her mouth grew strong. She fisted him with one hand and gently smoothed her thumb over his tip.

Not entirely confident in what she was doing, she leaned close. She'd given a blow job to Kirk a few times, but she'd been nervous. He'd reassured her, *the only bad blowjob is no blowjob.*

Lily hadn't felt good about it. Now, she closed her lips around Brandon. He growled as her tongue licked him and swirled the tip. She took him farther in, then sucked back to the top. He groaned and gripped one hand at the back of her neck. She repeated the movement, each time taking him a little farther, as much as she could.

"Fuck," he hissed through gritted teeth.

Her mouth and her fist now moved in concert, sucking him hard on the way up. Her own passion grew, and moisture accumulated between her legs.

"Shit. Lily, I don't want to come in your mouth." He held on to her shoulders and freed himself.

She looked up at his gorgeous brown eyes, now afire with passion. "But I was thirsty."

"Oh, you wicked woman, with that wicked mouth." Brandon needed to be inside Lily so badly his balls ached. And seeing her in a red lace bra and thong sent him over the edge. He lifted her and sealed his lips to hers, plunging his tongue into her warm, waiting mouth.

"I can't wait another moment." He'd never wanted a woman as much as he wanted Lily right then.

He unclipped the bra and pushed it off her shoulders, sending it to the floor. He backed her a few steps to the bed, saying, "Wait here." He retrieved a condom from his pants and covered himself.

He hooked his fingers around her thong, dragged it to the floor, and stood back. His eyes combed her body—her flushed cheeks, her hard cherry nipples, a smattering of silky hair over her mons. He savored the image. "Beautiful. Now, lie back."

She slid back on the bed, sprawled out for him. He rested his body over hers. Her lips apart, she panted gently. He wasted no time and claimed her mouth, sucking her bottom lip and tongue, tasting all he could of her. Her mouth was sweet against his, he didn't want to stop and yet he wanted more at the same time.

He knelt between her legs and dragged the tip of his dick along her wet pussy. She bowed off the bed and gasped. He played, watching and marveling at the beauty of her body and incredible responsiveness she had to his every touch.

He shifted his position and, one at a time, he lifted her legs to his shoulders. "You will feel me go deeper in this position. I will go slow, Lily. But remember what I told you yesterday. You will come. You will come with me. Okay?"

She nodded as he aligned himself with her opening and gently pushed in.

"Ah," she groaned, closing her eyes.

He focused on her—her hair fanned across the pillow, the smooth curve of her hips, the plump nipples on her delectable breasts—so he could capture this memory forever.

He began to pump into her, slowly at first, each time gaining more space for her to accommodate him. Her breathing sped, as did his.

"Ah." Her head shifted from side to side. "Brandon," she panted.

"Yes, baby." He kept his pace and added a finger, massaging her wonderfully hard nub.

He was so fucking close, and his balls drew tight to his body.

In several moments, moans spilled from her mouth unabashedly. "Oh, God, Brandon . . ." She gripped his forearms and cried out.

He pounded into her several more times and released his own climax. He pulled out and collapsed to her side, both of them panting as he recovered from the best damn orgasm of his life.

Fuck me! This was their last night, and he wished it would never end.

Chapter 7

BRANDON'S CELL PHONE rang the morning of Lily's departure for the States. He told her he would drive her to the airport and he wouldn't *accept no for an answer*.

She figured, what could it matter? This goodbye was already hard; it truly couldn't get any more gut-wrenching. She busied herself with a final sweep of the room, checking drawers and the closet, anything to occupy her mind.

". . . We're all well-aware of the new MDR . . . But Laurel isn't shipping any product into the EU . . . Christ . . . Yes. Fine. I'll be right there." He let out another expletive and shoved his phone in his suit jacket pocket.

"Lily," he raised his head to meet her gaze. His eyes read frustrated, anxious, and sad. "I can't drive you to the airport. I have to handle something with the Italian government. It should have been easy to manage, but it seems one of my people has upset an official," his voice dipped.

She was speechless. *This is it?*

He sighed and stepped closer. "I'm sorry."

She dug deep for a smile and forced it on her lips. "I completely understand. Go take care of business. I'll get a cab."

"Thank you." He leaned down to place a quick peck on her lips. "I won't forget these last four days. They've been incredible."

"For me, too."

He kissed her again, deeper this time. A goodbye kiss that would have to last for an eternity. It was sweet, but hot and demanding. God, his mouth. She may never get a kiss like that again. She wrapped her arms around his neck and he pulled her closer.

Then, just as she got caught up in it, he pulled back. He pecked her forehead, and with his hands on her shoulders, he said, "You sure you're okay getting a cab?"

She nodded. Words were lost on her as she just stared into his brown eyes.

"Okay. Take care of yourself, Lily."

He released her arms and turned for the door, and with a quick wave, he was gone. The door clicked closed, causing Lily to jump.

Lily stood, glaring at the door for who knows how long. He just left. A kiss, some parting words, and that was it.

Tears threatened to spill from her eyes. She knew what their interlude was about, and tears were not part of the plan. She'd fallen in love with him. He clearly didn't feel the same. And that's okay. It had to be okay. Because right about then, given enough time, she might crawl back into bed and wallow for the next few hours or next few days.

Time wasn't a luxury she had. She inhaled, pushed back her shoulders, gripped the handle on her suitcase, and after a final visual sweep of the room, she headed out the door.

Goodbye sweet, remodeled, but still old hotel room. Goodbye Rome. Goodbye sweet memories of the man who made her heart full, and then deflated it, all in the span of four simple days.

Chapter 8

THROWING HERSELF INTO work would be what she needed to keep her sanity. Lily needed distraction; getting her mind off Brandon would be the thing to save her from herself, from wallowing in her thoughts of him.

Adjusting to Pacific Time Zone took more out of her than usual, and she dared herself not to think it could attributed to Brandon.

She sat at her desk, her first official day back at work, when her cell phone rang. One glance at the screen of the smiling, dark-blonde with eyes like emeralds and she knew who it was.

"Lil! You're back! How was Italy?" Courtney's energetic voice bellowed over the phone.

"Hey, Court. It was fine."

"It was fine. That's it?"

"Mmmhmm."

Lily could practically hear Courtney's wheels turning.

"You don't sound like yourself. What's wrong?"

"I'm still jet-lagged, I think." She sighed.

Courtney paused for a few beats.

"You've been there a million times. Most times when you return I'm getting a ton of details about everything you saw and did. What gives? Something happened. Were you laid off already? Did Kirk call?"

How to tell her best friend? Her trip to Italy had been the most amazing four days of her life. What started as hot sex had turned into something more. She surprised herself at how quickly she'd been drawn to Brandon, how he'd lowered her guard and gotten past her emotional defenses. He'd treated her better than any other man—as if she were special—and she hadn't expected that in a short-term fling.

"Kirk is history. I met someone."

"Yeah? An Italian?" Courtney's smile vibrated through the phone.

"No, an American."

"Really? So, what happened? Isn't that good news?" Her voice pitched with excitement.

"Not exactly. He lives in Miami, so very little chance of seeing him again." Not that Lily expected that. She was very much "girl next door", and he was more "GQ cover model". Plus his goodbye told her he didn't feel the way she did. She'd fallen for Brandon, hard. And for him, she was merely the flavor of the week.

She sighed. Anytime she thought about Brandon she missed him and her heart ached.

"You really liked this guy, didn't you?" Courtney asked softly.

Lily had fallen in love with Brandon. But he didn't love her.

"Yes, I think I did."

"So what are you going to do?"

"What can I do? I need to forget about it." *Easier said than done.*

Now it was Courtney's turn to sigh. "Wrecked emotions."

"You got that right."

Lily promised her friend the rest of the details, but not at work. It may be wishful thinking, but Lily hoped there was still a chance she'd get to keep her job. They wrapped up their phone conversation, and Courtney vowed a super-size pitcher of sangria after work to help her forget about her "gorgeous hunk with the great lips."

No small surprise, four days after returning to LA from Rome, she got called into Human Resources. The HR rep looked like she'd already had one hell of a day and it was barely eleven.

Lily would be among the many to get laid off from ALK. But dammit! Three full days! They knew she'd returned; they could have done this earlier. That gave her false hope that she wasn't getting laid-off after all.

What a slap in the face! She worked harder these last few days, added more detail to her reports from Italy, including additional recommendations for the rose hip farm.

She held back her tears, and with her severance package in hand, she dropped a box on her desk to pack her things. She'd have time to cry tonight.

The buzz of her phone caught her attention. A voicemail.

She retrieved it, and that rich, soothing voice she loved so much played in her ear. Brandon. Her heart nearly leapt out of her chest.

Lily. Hi, it's Brandon. I hope you made it home safely. I . . . I just wanted to check in on you and tell you again how much I enjoyed spending time with you. I'm back in the States and would love to get together again, if your schedule permits. I can fly out there or I could send you a ticket to come to Miami. Call me back, okay? Take care.

God, hearing his voice instantly sent her to heaven. The memories of Rome, of the time she shared with him, flooded her entire body. Lily glanced upward with the prickly sensation in her eyes, and her fists clenched.

DO. NOT. CRY. AT. WORK.

As exciting as the phone call from Brandon was, it was equally horrible. How could she forget about him after hearing his sexy voice?

He wanted to see her again, but why?

Brandon was some kind of top-notch executive. She didn't even know his job title, but she knew he was a bigwig. Born of parents of average means, where coupons were clipped and family vacations were an exercise of how-much-can-we-cram-in, she lacked the sophistication of his world. He had to know she didn't run in those circles, so why was he calling her?

Sex. That could be the only answer. Because a man like Brandon could have any—polished and cultured—woman he wanted. Getting caught up in some sense of obligation to her would only tie him down. Lily wouldn't stand in the way of his work or more importantly of his finding a woman appropriate to his social standing.

She bit down on her cheek so hard she tasted blood. Staring at her phone, she did the only thing she could do—she deleted the message.

She sat numbly for several minutes. God that hurt. The knot in her stomach weighted her like lead.

Could this day get any worse? She stroked a finger under each eye and tried to focus on her packing. Time to put on her big girl panties and start her job search.

Forget about him and move on, Lil.

***

How he'd fucked up! Days had passed and Brandon hadn't heard a single word from Lily since Rome. No small wonder that she wouldn't call him back or return his texts. Italy had been all about sex. He'd made it all about sex. Sure, there were moments that felt very much like a *relationship.* In fact, he'd never felt more at ease with a woman, or truly engaged in a conversation with a woman he was also attracted to than he had with Lily. But he'd never told her that.

Why would she return a 3,000-mile booty-call? Even though it wasn't a booty-call. He rubbed the heels of his hands against his eyes. *Dammit!*

At her hotel room that last morning, he'd panicked. His phone rang and he jumped to it, using it as an excuse to avoid a heavy conversation. One of those feelings that he didn't want to admit to. The hollow look in her eyes nearly ripped a hole in his heart. He had no experience in this area, but his gut told him he should have handled it better.

And now he sat in his German car, under a palm tree, a block down from his parents' house, vowing to regain composure before Sunday dinner. If he hadn't screwed things up with Lily, maybe she'd be coming to dinner with him.

Brandon strolled into the spacious kitchen expecting to see both parents and his sisters. Vegetables, pots and pans, and various spices filled the counter space where his mother worked. Mom gave the cook the weekends off. She secretly loved to cook for her family, and Sunday dinner was always a highlight of her week.

"Hi, Mom. Where is everyone?"

"Brandon, you made it." She wiped her hands on a towel and hugged him. He leaned down to kiss her cheek. "Your sisters will be along soon. Your father is on the phone with Burt, planning his next golf game," she said with a grin.

His mother had soft skin, glowing blue eyes, and looked ten years younger than her age. If it weren't for the gray hiding in her blonde hair, she might even look twenty years younger.

"Sit. I'm just finishing the vegetables. Tell me about Rome." She beamed at him.

He retrieved a wine glass from the cabinet and poured a hefty portion of merlot.

Where to start? He slid onto a barstool at the island where his mother operated. "It went well. Corticelli will be a great acquisition. And most of their people seem on board."

She glanced up from her preparations at him. "Most?"

He smiled to keep it light. "I had some pushback from their lead attorney, but I think things are straightened out now. What he failed to realize was that unless there was some regulation we were violating, this merger was going through."

She nodded and eyed him again. "I see." She paused a beat. "Brandon, is there something else? You look tired."

This was not the conversation he wanted to have right then.

"I'm fine, Mom. Still getting over jetlag."

She let out an exhale, and stopped cooking to turn his direction. "Son, please take it easy. I'm concerned you work too much."

Oh, here we go.

"Working hard is what gave your father a heart attack." Her voice softened. "Our lives are forever changed. I'm so grateful he survived, but nevertheless things are different. I don't want anything to happen to you—be careful."

He reached for her hand, clasping it in his. "I will, Mom."

"Maybe you need a girlfriend. A reason to cut back on your hours."

Brandon shrugged. He had only one girl on his mind.

"You're too handsome *not* to have a girlfriend," she said while seasoning the Cuban pulled pork.

He rolled his eyes. "Mom, you're a little biased."

"I'm not the only one who thinks so, otherwise they wouldn't have put you on the cover of *Miami Monthly.*"

He shook his head and grinned.

"But I'm serious, Brandon. You work too much."

He peered at her and saw the sincerity and concern in her eyes. "I'll be fine, Mom."

Brandon didn't consider himself to be like his father. He took care of himself better—he went to the gym, avoided excessive sugar, and drank in moderation. His father had worked too hard, never went to a gym, sometimes drank too much, and for a few years, had smoked cigars.

"That's what your father told me a million times." *Oh, shit!*

As she went back to her task, she started in again. "Your father's heart attack was both a blessing and a curse. You may not know this, but years ago we almost divorced."

That was news to him. He shifted in his seat.

"He was forced to stop working, and since then our marriage has never been better. All I'm saying is at least think about cutting back." She leveled him with a penetrating stare.

"Okay, Mom."

He agreed that his parents seemed to be doing well; early retirement became both of them. But cutting back on office hours might not be entirely possible. Besides, it was just the distraction Brandon needed to take his mind off Lily, if only for brief moments at a time.

As everyone loaded their plates with fare—black beans and rice, plantains, mojo sauce for the pulled pork, the conversation started. Brandon wondered how long it would take for his father to ask about Laurel. His father may be retired, but he built this company from nothing but a dream. He'd rented a small office space from a friend and steadily grew it to a profitable, thriving business. He couldn't completely divest himself of Laurel. Probably never would—and Brandon understood.

"So the Corticelli acquisition's moving forward?" His father asked from the head of the table as he speared a bite of pulled pork.

Without fail, every eye turned to Brandon. His sisters already knew the details; Brandon had briefed them upon his return. They ran the company in his absence and had filled him in on what transpired while he was away. On paper, he was in charge, but behind the scenes the three of them made most of the decisions together.

"Yes, all things are proceeding as planned. We will lay some ground work, but hold off on final execution until after the move."

"How's that going?" his mother asked.

"Good," Katie chimed in. "The lobby is getting remodeled now, some offices need updating. I have a meeting next week with Caliber to get infrastructure plans down on paper, plus the city will want to do their inspection." She smiled. "And naturally Tim and I will be looking for houses."

Tim was Katie's fiancé, and the person responsible for selling Brandon on moving Laurel headquarters to Texas. Tim would say with a chuckle, *There's no ocean-flooding in Dallas, Brandon.* Brandon had had enough of the water damage caused to the offices, the lab, and sometimes even manufacturing. Even with flood insurance, he and his sisters agreed, a more suitable, long-term solution was necessary.

"Great, let me know if you see anything I'd like. I had zero time to look while I was out there," Brandon requested.

She lifted her eyebrows. "Like I'm supposed to know what you'd like."

Leena piped up. "Just look for anything big and plain, and in a neighborhood that has no kids."

Mom covered her laugh with her hand, and Katie chuckled. "Oh, so a rich boy's bachelor pad? That's easy."

And they all laughed at his expense. "Very funny, you two."

He smiled, because it *was* funny. The old Brandon would want a house or condo just like they described. What he couldn't tell anyone was that he'd give his left arm to share that house with Lily.

Over dinner, the Morgans discussed Katie's upcoming wedding, Leena's new deck, and surprisingly little more discussion of Laurel Med. Brandon and his sisters made discreet eye contact over their father's ability not to pry further into company business. Not that they minded. They'd come to expect it. But how things had changed for their parents. They looked happy, peaceful. His father made a conscience effort to make changes in his life and clearly it was paying off.

Chapter 9

BRANDON'S APARTMENT FELT void of any life. An otherwise spacious, contemporary condo on the beach, he hadn't realized how blank the walls were. He should have purchased some art when he moved in. Instead a vastness of stark white stared back at him, daring him to do something.

He massaged his brow.

He underestimated what Lily had come to mean to him. He tried to minimize their relationship to just sex, and why? To protect the company? Or to protect himself? If he gathered a moment of brutal honesty, he would give up the company in a heartbeat, throw it all away, for a lifetime with Lily.

And that shocked the shit out of him.

It was probably for the best that she'd dropped out of his life. He was really doing her a favor. He worked too damn much to give the proper attention to a woman like Lily. She deserved to be cherished, adored, loved, and respected. In some alternate universe he was exactly the man for the job. But right then, with a company to run, stockholders to answer to, a corporate move to complete, an acquisition to execute, and a family counting on him? No. He had no time for a relationship. Hell, he barely had time for his friendships, never mind a romance.

Brandon stared blankly out his condo window. He replayed the conversation with his mother. She told Brandon he was in denial. That he worked just as hard as his father and stress kills.

Lily would be his reason to cut back on hours at work.

He glanced one last time at his cell phone screen. Nothing. Since he'd returned from his trip, he'd called Lily twice and texted her three times. He told himself he could text her one last time, and that was it. If she didn't reply, he had his answer: she didn't want to see him. He wouldn't search for her; he would let it be.

He opened the message program and began:

Lily, this will be my final text, if you want it to be. I won't bother you anymore.

Please know in the short time we were together, you've come to mean a lot to me. I miss you, and I pray you will call me or text me back. Brandon

***

Job prospects for Lily were few and far between. She was either too qualified, not the right fit, or flat-out not interested. One position, she'd come to learn, was project manager plus occasional receptionist duties. *What?*

Courtney referred a reputable headhunter to her. Lily had a face-to-face meeting with the man, and they hit it off. He was sharp as hell. She only hoped the headhunter could find something good for her.

To keep her mind off Brandon, she spent more time at the beach, snagged Groupons for yoga classes, and watched Netflix with Courtney.

Lily's curiosity got the better of her one day. She searched "Brandon Morgan". Her eyes were immediately drawn to the picture of Brandon, looking handsome as ever in a tuxedo, arm in arm with a tall blonde woman. Her hair was perfect, her skin was perfect, her teeth were perfect—the antithesis of Lily.

Her gut twisted at the image of the two of them.

See! You are not his type.

She couldn't look a moment longer. She closed out of the browser and slammed down the lid of her laptop. Lily swore to keep her Internet research to job-related stuff only. Her emotions couldn't handle anything beyond that.

In the midst of all this, Brandon had tried contacting her several times. One call came through while she sat at her little kitchen table eating left-overs. She stared at her phone as it rang and vibrated against her plate. It took all her strength not to pick up that call. She literally had her hand over the phone, and the ache in her heart was excruciating. Tears streamed down her face. The ringing eventually stopped. A sob escaped, and she sat alone, praying the thoughts and memories would just stop.

In her dreams, she was the kind of woman to complement him—thin, statuesque, from money. In reality, she was a full-figured thirty-year old with twelve thousand dollars in her retirement account, worried about when she'd land her next job.

Chapter 10

MONTHS PASSED AND Laurel's new headquarters looked and functioned like the Fortune 1000 company it was. The corporate move went as smoothly as could be expected. The twenty-story building located in downtown Dallas had more technological advances and efficiencies than their Miami building, which was a refreshing change. The Corticelli paperwork finalized the prior week, so that transition would soon be underway. Brandon moved into a condo in a secure building close to the office; those were his main two requirements and little else mattered.

All this progress and one thing left him unsettled—he had no word from Lily.

Multiple times he considered tracking her down. He knew where she worked, it wouldn't be that difficult. But she clearly didn't want to see him, so he vowed to move on.

One big change? He pledged to delegate more. The desire to fill his father's shoes, living up to expectations, weighed heavily on him. He, Katie, and Leena spent a Saturday afternoon at his Dallas condo, restructuring some responsibilities, revising chains of command, and generally cutting the excess that didn't align with the company's vision or their personal goals.

"And while we're at it," Katie pushed a sheet paper across the table to him, "call one of these decorators. You cannot live in boring bachelor pads any longer, Bran. You're thirty-six. Time to grow up," she said with a loving smile.

Leena nodded and covered his hand with hers. "This will be a great move, Bran."

He may have lost Lily, but his mother and sisters were right. He'd need to change a few things in his life or create a life for himself full of nothing but regrets.

***

"Hey, Lil. You need this other black heel?" Courtney asked with her hand held high.

The headhunter had contacted Lily regarding an interview with a firm in Dallas. The position was for project manager and the pay was excellent. Few details were available, although the recruiter made it clear that if she was offered, and accepted the job, Lily would need to move to Dallas. The last time she went to Dallas, she'd met Brandon on her lay-over to Rome.

Don't think about him.

She peered out of her bathroom to look at which shoe Court had and cringed. "Yeah."

"What are you doing?"

"I can't find my new lipstick. Whatever." She rifled through her cosmetic bag one last time in search of the stupid lipstick. It was just a drugstore brand, but it complimented her pale skin. Made her look more sophisticated.

"You're nervous, aren't you?"

She walked into her bedroom and sighed. "Yes, I think I am."

"Don't be. They're gonna love you. I just don't know what I'll do when you have to move."

Sure, LA was home. She'd moved there with her parents right before she turned ten. She loved so much about the town—the clubs, the energy, beach on one side, mountains on the other—but since her trip to Italy, her hometown had lost its appeal. Her parents spent more time at their vacation home in Arizona, the goal to eventually retire there. Aside from a few close friends, she had nothing tying her to LA, so she eagerly accepted the interview.

"Hey, I haven't even interviewed yet. No discussion of moving until then."

Lily would miss Courtney to death, but by the same token, a fresh start could be good. Free of ALK, and free of the job that brought Brandon into her life. Free of Kirk. Free of plastic people with plastic bodies. The opportunity to start over, make something great of her life, like Courtney said, was calling her.

Chapter 11

BRANDON LEFT HIS comptroller's office and strolled across the sixteenth floor reception area to the elevator. His new headquarters with huge glass windows, chrome accents, dark wood floors and contemporary art was something to be proud of. His mind raced with things still left to accomplish, but all-in-all the move went well.

If it could just be enough to make him forget Lily.

"Good morning, Mr. Morgan."

"Good morning, Penny," he replied as he strode toward the elevator, heading to his office on the twentieth floor.

The silhouette of a woman sitting in the reception area caught his eye. Shoulder-length brown wavy hair, navy suit, and navy heels. He paused. Her head rose. She saw him and froze as her jaw dropped.

Lily sat in the sixteenth-floor reception of *his* new corporate headquarters.

She looked exactly as he remembered—shiny brunette hair, bright eyes, shapely legs. Beautiful. Maybe even more so. His heart hammered in his chest.

He quickly deduced she was there to be interviewed. He ignored the elevator door that sounded as it opened, and briskly pivoted on his heel toward the receptionist.

"Penny, who is Miss Bennett interviewing with?"

Smiling brightly, she scanned her computer screen.

He glanced at Lily to see she tracked his every movement.

"Uh, looks like Tom Ashley, sir," Penny replied.

"Let Tom know I'm going to meet with her briefly, and I'll bring her to him right after that."

"Yes, sir."

He strode over to Lily, and loomed for several seconds. Thoughts surged through his mind, but he didn't know where to start.

"Miss Bennett, would you kindly follow me?" He winced. His voice was curt from the adrenaline flooding his blood stream.

The elevator ride was silent as he bore a hole into her, not believing she stood before him, *months* after their time together in Italy.

She eyed him from beneath her lashes, nibbled on her bottom lip, and fidgeted with her portfolio. She was adorable as ever.

"Donna, I'd like to be undisturbed for a few minutes." His assistant looked up from her computer at her over-sized cubicle located outside his office. Donna was efficient and smart, and Brandon thanked the angels above that she agreed to move to Dallas with the company.

"Yes, sir."

He guided Lily into his office and closed the door behind him. There was nothing to interrupt them, no glass walls to steal their attention, and yet he stood in his spacious office, staring at the woman that filled his thoughts day and night, and he couldn't form a coherent thought.

She looked at him with her blue eyes wide, part from nervousness and part from surprise, like him.

Brandon unbuttoned his suit jacket and shoved his hands in his pants' pockets. "Why didn't you return my calls?" He sounded like a petulant child, but he didn't care. Both anger and relief flooded his psyche in equal measure. But hell, he was finally in the same room with her.

Her cheeks filled with pink before she glanced down.

He leaned against his desk, trying not to appear so imposing. "Lily?"

"I don't know." She slipped her hair behind her ear. "Why didn't you tell me you work here?"

He thought he had at some point. "I guess it didn't come up."

Her heels shifted on the carpet, and she stared at him, unease written all over her face.

"What's going on, Lily?" Was she intimidated? Or hiding something? "Do you have a boyfriend?"

She scoffed. "No." Her chest rose with a breath. "Brandon, let's get real. You lived in Miami and I in LA. The distance alone isn't conducive for building a relationship. Besides, someone like you doesn't get seriously involved with someone like me."

"What?"

She exhaled. "You are a billionaire. I have a billfold. We live at opposite ends of the spectrum, Brandon."

He furrowed his brow. "That's why you didn't call me back?" *Unbelievable.*

He ran a hand through his hair. This was his chance, and he couldn't blow it. He would say what should have been said months ago. He took her portfolio out of her grasp and rested it on his desk, then held both of her hands in his. "Lily, I owe you an apology. Multiple apologies."

She blinked twice.

"What we had in Italy was more than a fling. I let you believe it was only sex, and for that I'm sorry. I could tell it was more, but I denied it. You are an amazing woman, and I should have told you. And not right after fucking you."

She blushed.

"I also want to apologize for how I left it. Would you at least have dinner with me tonight? We could talk, and after that if you still want nothing to do with me, you can leave and never look back."

Brandon stood, his warm hands wrapped around hers, his presence filling the immense space. As it always had. Brandon was larger than life, confident, handsome, yet sweet and real. She paled in comparison—her Ann Taylor off-the-rack versus his custom Italian fine wool suit.

God, he was beautiful. Her knees wobbled. Even after all these months apart, he could still turn her to jelly.

She pushed her shoulders back. "I'm interviewing for a job at your company," was the best she could come up with.

"All the better," he said with a smile. "You're interviewing for a lead project manager position, right?"

"Yes."

"I had you in mind when I told the team to open the requisition for the position."

Her heart pounded in her chest.

"The way you work seamlessly between businesswoman to confidante. The employees never see it coming. They are comfortable around you, and want to please you. That's exactly what I'm looking for to manage the Corticelli acquisition."

"What?" She yanked her hands back. As if her nerves weren't already on edge . . . the merger?

The headhunter had given her sketchy details of the job, but with few job prospects on the horizon and the salary being offered, she *had* no choice but to at least give it a shot. Her palms went slick. "But I don't know anything about buying a foreign company, or transitioning—"

He reached for her hand. "All that stuff doesn't matter, Lily. I have a team for all the legalese. What I don't have is someone intimately familiar with Italian customs. I want this to be a smooth transition. I don't want to risk morale taking a dive, or attrition going sky-high. You are perfect." He tipped his head. "Please interview. Don't make a decision based on me. On us."

Her stomach turned over multiple times. He'd created this position with her in mind? Lily began to doubt if she was merely just a plaything for him. But the project manager on a major corporate acquisition? *Shit!*

Her mind blurred. She was definitely in over her head, on many levels.

She shook her head slowly, bemused. "I don't know, Brandon."

"You will be great. Talk to Tom yourself. You'll see.

He lifted her hand to his lips for a small kiss. "Regardless of whether you take the job or not, have dinner with me tonight."

Her return flight to LA wasn't for another day, but still. She shrugged her shoulder.

He stepped around his large desk and grabbed a notepad and pen, scribbling something on it. He ripped off the page and handed it to her. "Please take this. This is my address. But I'll have a car drive you. The bellman will let you into my apartment. Wait for me there after your interviews. Please."

Her head swam with a million questions.

Months of thinking and dreaming about him, and here he stood before her, CEO of a company she was interviewing with.

She knew when she'd left Italy, she'd lost her heart. And neither time nor space diminished that emotion. Memories consumed her.

Courtney's voice played in her head, *what do you have to lose?* She inhaled and nodded in agreement.

He smiled, his gaze suddenly penetrating her. "If you didn't have your interview, I'd kiss you senseless right now."

Oh God! He kissed the back of her hand and released it.

"I'll see you tonight. Make yourself at home." He proceeded to the door, and opening it, he called out, "Donna, would you escort Miss Bennett to Tom Ashley's office?"

"Yes, sir."

"Thank you."

Lily concentrated on every step she took to retrieve her portfolio and walk toward him.

"Good luck."

"Thank you," she breathed. She would need it after that unexpected interlude.

Chapter 12

A DRIVER GREETED Lily at the lobby of Laurel Med headquarters to take her to Brandon's condo. After three interviews, she was drained, but in a good way. The company was truly amazing. Cutting-edge, innovative, and good to its employees. Although it was larger than ALK, Lily could imagine working for this company, comfortably fitting in.

As the bellman opened Brandon's condo door, the sight of two dozen, long-stemmed red roses in a crystal vase on a coffee table greeted her immediately. Her mind instantly went back to Rome, when he'd sent her flowers. They were breathtaking.

"Anything else, Miss?" the bellman asked.

The turn of events nearly had her running for the door. Before her interview, the man she'd longed for and denied herself, told her in so many words he wanted to be with her.

"No. Thank you."

The door closed, and she stood in place, taking in the spacious home and looking for Brandon in it. Clean, sleek and contemporary. The living room held a large black leather sofa and two leather chairs with a glass and metal cocktail table directly center. A ginormous TV hung on the wall facing the sofa, and soft gray linen drapes hung open over a wall of windows. At the opposite end, the room spilled into the open kitchen with a sleek, dark wood dining table.

She set her coat, purse, and portfolio on a chair, and walked to the cocktail table to inhale the rose scent hovering in the air. On the white walls hung several abstract oil paintings on canvas. She walked the space some more. There were very few personal items about. A few books stacked on an end table with a remote, and the *Wall Street Journal* was on the floor in front of the table as if he'd lost interest in the article.

She focused on what appeared to be family photos—his parents and his two sisters, Katie and Leena—blonde just like their mother. Brandon evidently got his thick brown hair from his father. They looked like a close family, and Lily had to smile. A ping of jealousy, seeing the siblings, shot through her. She had no complaints about her life, but more than once she wondered what it would be like to have a brother or sister. Wondered if they would be close like Brandon and his sisters appeared to be.

One photo caught her eye. She squinted and moved closer to a photo of Brandon and one of his sisters. *Ohmigod!* That was the woman she saw when she searched the Internet some time ago. She'd automatically assumed it was a girlfriend, but she'd been wrong.

Lily gently shook her head and spun around to roam more of the space. The powder bath painted in a rich lavender was situated to the left and a large bedroom, likely a guest room, in pale gray to the right. The attention to detail, like each item was selected to play well with all the items in the rooms, left little doubt a designer had decorated Brandon's condo. It had a good flow and everything looked expensive.

She proceeded to the end of the hall to find Brandon's bedroom.

She gasped. Her eye was immediately drawn to the painting over the king bed with a lustrous dark headboard. A beautiful, large oil painting of a sunset over vast green fields lined with tall juniper trees stared at her. *Siena.*

She cupped a hand over her heart.

What if she read it all wrong? What if he felt the way she did?

She absently glossed her fingertips over the dark gray duvet. Everything he owned felt luxurious. She slowly shook her head. How could she *fit* into his world?

She stepped back. "I need a glass of wine," she told the inanimate object.

She strode to the subzero refrigerator, found an already opened bottle of chardonnay and popped off the cork.

She exhaled as she sat at the dining table. For a successful CEO, Brandon had a modest ego. Sometimes he was all "take charge", but others, laid-back and easy going. She liked both sides of him. In Italy, though, she could tell he hadn't revealed himself entirely to her. Hence, she was just now learning he was a CEO of a large international company.

But she knew for certain she'd caught glimpses of the real Brandon—the thoughtful, easy going, barriers-down gentleman who had treated her like a goddess.

Her mind wandered to the job at his company. If she didn't get the job, not that she suspected Brandon would let that happen, how could they still have a long-distance relationship?

If she got an offer, she would move to Dallas and work for him. The pay beyond her wildest dreams. This move would be amazing for her career. But what of Brandon? How appropriate was it to fraternize with the boss? *Is that ethical?*

Shit! She gulped some of her wine.

"What are you thinking?"

She jumped in her seat. "Oh Brandon, I didn't hear you." Lily looked up at the man constantly in her thoughts, now physically just ten feet away. He smiled gently at her, loosening his red tie.

"I wasn't trying to sneak up on you," he said. "You were deep in thought." He moved to the chair opposite from where she sat and took off his jacket, hanging it on the back of a chair. "What were you thinking about?"

She decided to be honest. "You."

Suddenly, the place, so well appointed, everything hand-selected, came alive because Brandon was in it. She could practically feel the energy radiating off him. For her, it was a calming energy.

He slipped his hands in his pants pockets. "That's good. Anything you'd like to share?"

She shrugged her shoulders. "Maybe later."

"How did the interview go?"

"It went well. They asked if I could meet with someone else tomorrow."

"What did you say?"

"I said yes."

He nodded, looking serious and pensive. "Mind if I join you?"

She motioned to the chair.

As he poured a glass of wine, he positioned himself in a chair across from her. Now she wanted to know what he was thinking.

The air was thick between them. So much to say, and yet she wasn't sure where to start.

"You go by Brandon, why?"

He glanced down with a grin. "I had four Mikes in my kindergarten class, and my teacher, who was like a hundred, asked us to change our names for her sanity."

She smiled, picturing Brandon as a boy, running around with friends, organizing a game with teams and rules, yet confident his team would win.

"I think about Rome a lot," he began. "Do you?"

Her gaze shot to the roses on the sofa table. "Yes."

"And you. I had a hard time getting you out of my head." He exhaled. "Can you deny that Italy was incredible?"

She shook her head. "No, it was. Probably the best four days of my life," she murmured. She felt the prickling in her eyes and willed the tears to stay. "But Brandon, you and I both know I'm not *really* your type. A tall, thin model needs to be on your arm."

She hated letting her insecurities show, and she would deal with that later. Right now, she needed open, honest communication. Time to put her feelings out there.

His eyes narrowed. He sat for another few moments—it felt like an eternity—before rising to walk to her. He took her hand, gently tugged, and she stood.

He wrapped his hands around hers. "As you can clearly see, I'm not with any woman like what you've described. At thirty-six, I think I have a good idea of what I want in a woman, and fake women do not impress me." He dropped his gaze to their hands and his thumb circled over her hand. "Maybe it was fate that I walked into your hotel room that night. Because you are exactly what I want in my life, and I didn't even know it."

Her eyes grew watery.

"I walked out of your hotel room that morning believing you would be easy to forget. I was so very wrong." He pressed his lips together. "Regardless of whether you take this job, I'm going to see you, Lily. I'm going to fly to wherever you are. We are going to get to know each other until you are comfortable with *us*. We'll take as much time as you need for you to realize you're supposed to move here to Dallas and be with me." His lips curved convincingly.

Her stomach turned over, and her heart thumped in her chest. Was she hearing him right? He wanted her. Wanted to be with her. Truly. "You're crazy."

He leaned down and gently kissed her lips, nibbled, and kissed more. "Crazy about you," he said softly.

His hands clasped her face as he claimed her mouth with passion. His firm lips and soft tongue owned her. Her knees weakened the longer the kiss went on. She leaned into him, wanting to feel more of him, needing more.

His hardness pressed into her, and all the wonderful memories came rushing back. She wrapped her arms around his neck and laced her fingers through his hair. The wetness accumulated at the apex of her thighs.

"Lily. I want you more than anything or anyone I've wanted in my life. I want to take you here," he said as he pushed the placemats off the table onto the floor.

He was asking for her permission. His face strained as he awaited her answer. This was a crucial point in what could be a relationship, a long-term relationship with Brandon. Maybe lust clouded her brain, but if she could believe his words, he was ready to commit to her, and for all the right reasons.

Her tongue swiped over her lips. She reached for the hem of her skirt, scrunched it in her hands to unveil her panties. She slipped her thumbs under the waistband, dragged the lacy confection to the floor and stepped out.

His dick surged in his pants. *Fuck!* "God, Lily." He cupped her jaw and kissed her fiercely. He dove into her mouth with the hunger of a starving man. She wrapped her arms around him. Those same delicate arms he felt months ago. It's as if time stood still for them.

Finally he pushed back to release his pants and sheath himself with a condom he'd dug out of his back pocket. She hoisted up her skirt and wiggled her hips on the table. He maneuvered between her legs and held her face with one hand, smoothing a thumb over her cheek. With his free hand, Brandon stroked himself gently through her slit, testing.

He stared deeply into her eyes. "Know this. I'm falling for you—your body *and* your mind. As much as you'll have me, I want you."

"Oh God." Her breath came rapidly and her beautiful cheeks filled with pink.

Then he drove into her and she cried out.

"I missed you, Brandon." She panted and moved with him. "I thought about you every day."

"I missed you." He kissed her and breathed over her lips, "Be with me, Lily. We're good together. Say you'll give us a chance."

"I will."

He smiled before he plunged deeper into her, giving her all he could, and eager to give her everything.

But wait, there's more. Look for **Undeniable Love** coming soon!

Thank you for reading!

If you enjoyed this story, please consider posting a review at one or more of your favorite retailers. Even a short review, one or two lines, can be a tremendous encouragement to the author. Your review is also a gift to other readers who may be searching for just this sort of story and will be grateful that you helped them find it.

Thank you!

Other Books by Mia London

Life To The Max
Wanton Angel, Prequel to Life To The Max
Perfect Seduction (Perfect, 1)
Perfect Surrender (Perfect, 2)
Beyond Lace (Hard Men of the Rockies, 4)

ABOUT THE AUTHOR

Mia London loves to write.
After reading fiction for years, she decided it was finally time to put those images and scenes floating around in her head down on paper.

She is a huge fan of romance, highly optimistic, and wildly faithful to the HEA (happily ever after). Her goal is to create a fantasy you will enjoy with characters you could love.

She lives in Texas with her attentive, loving, super-model husband, and perfectly behaved, brilliant children. Her produce never wilts, there are no weeds in her flowerbeds and chocolate is her favorite food group.

Facebook
Twitter
Goodreads
Webpage
Email: **mia@mialondon.com**

www.ingramcontent.com/pod-product-compliance
Lightning Source LLC
Chambersburg PA
CBHW071132100726
47908CB00008B/2576